D0275516

A STORMY
GREEK MARRIAGE

A STORMY GREEK MARRIAGE

BY

LYNNE GRAHAM

MILLS & BOON

First published in Great Britain 2010
Large Print edition 2011
Harlequin Mills & Boon Limited,
Eton House, 18-24 Paradise Road,
Richmond, Surrey TW9 1SR

© Lynne Graham 2010

ISBN: 978 0 263 21563 2

Harlequin Mills & Boon policy is to use papers that are
natural, renewable and recyclable products and made
from wood grown in sustainable forests. The logging and
manufacturing process conform to the legal environmental
regulations of the country of origin.

Printed and bound in Great Britain
by CPI Antony Rowe, Chippenham, Wiltshire

CHAPTER ONE

THE opulent cloakroom was adorned with stylish contemporary fittings and fresh flower arrangements and was as large as many reception rooms. At a vanity unit that was more private than any of the others on offer, the bride was touching up her smudged eye makeup with a careful hand, while scolding herself for getting so weepy and overcome at the altar. However, her green eyes also shone with happiness. She jumped when the door from the hall noisily opened to feed in a burst of animated chattering females.

'…Calisto threw tantrums, so clearly Alexei decided that life would be easier with a doormat,' a very correct English voice pronounced with a giggle. 'He will get bored *so* fast—'

'And she's just a worker from his office… Who ever would have believed that a Drakos would even have looked at her?' someone else observed acidly.

'And *so* plain—positively dumpy!' the first speaker added with vitriol. 'As for *that* dress. No train and all that fussy dated embroidery. Obviously Alexei is on the rebound—'

Gritting her teeth together and keeping herself out of view, Billie was literally trying to mentally seal her ears and stop listening to the bitchy comments. She reflected in disbelief on the exquisite hand-embroidered heirloom dress that she had fallen madly in love with, feeling affronted and hurt by that criticism of her gown. She could have put a face to every voice though. All three women featured on Alexei's impossibly long list of former lovers, each of whom had gone on to marry or move in with one of his wealthy friends or business colleagues and thus contrived to stay within his social circle.

'Calisto must have really screwed up—a billionaire on the rebound. If I'd known that miracle was on the horizon, I'd have gone for a divorce and made myself available!' the Englishwoman

confided in a petulant tone that implied her outrageous suggestion was far from being a joke.

'But Calisto was a one-off,' her companion returned crushingly. 'She's the only one of Alexei's
exes that he's ever revisited.'

'What's that worth now when he's just married
right out of his class and culture? I give this mis-
matched union three months, four if she plays
her cards right and ignores it when he strays,'
the Englishwoman forecast. 'Then Alexei will
ditch his homely little bride so hard and fast her
head will spin!'

That was the exact moment when a glint
of defiant green flared in Billie's eyes. Pride
would not allow her to skulk out of sight somewhere in the splendid villa that was now her
home. As she moved into view three female
faces froze in a rictus of almost comical discomfiture. Sidestepping their stilled figures,
her bright auburn head held high, Billie left the
cloakroom.

Hilary, her aunt, was walking in circles in the
hall while she rocked the sobbing baby in her

arms. Her eyes settled on Billie in some relief. 'I've been looking everywhere for you. Nicky just won't settle for me. I think he's getting another tooth—'

'Let me take him.' Billie sped over immediately to grasp the little but solid, squirming body of her baby son. Her *secret* son, she reminded herself guiltily, gazing down worriedly into his cross little face. She adored him, wanted to show him off, not behave as though he were Hilary's child and her infant cousin. But that masquerade had been forced on her when she chose to bring Nicky and her aunt back with her to the island of Speros, for she had yet to tell the man she had just married that morning that she had conceived a child by him on the night following his parents' funeral. Unhappily, Alexei, having suffered a fall and a blow to the head shortly afterwards, had no memory of their brief intimacy. Their son's face was flushed below his spiky shock of silky black hair. She hugged him close in spite of her aunt's exhortations for her to be careful of her wedding gown. The scent and feel of the baby in her arms was a comfort to her frayed nerves and the charm seemed to work both ways because Nicky started to simmer down and indeed began to snuggle into his mother's soothing embrace.

A tall, devastatingly handsome, black-haired, olive-skinned male strode across the echoing hall towards Billie and Hilary. Instantly, all Billie's senses went on red alert and she sucked in a ragged breath to steady herself. She collided with Alexei's dark-lashed exotic bronzed eyes and her surroundings became immediately invisible: his effect on her was that shocking and intense. Her mouth ran dry because she could still barely credit that she was now his wife. That was a dream so long held and suppressed by her that even on her wedding day it could only seem to her to consist more of fantasy than fact. Alexei, blithely ignoring the greetings of those who would have sought to deflect him from his bride, drew level with her.

For a split second he seemed to stare at the sight of Billie cradling a child in her arms and his attention lingered on the striking contrast of the baby's tawny complexion and black hair against Billie's white dress, auburn hair and naturally pale skin. It struck him as surprising that the kid bore not the slightest resemblance to any one of his female relatives. A slight frown line forming between his sleek ebony brows, he dismissed that fleeting thought and snapped an imperious set of long fingers to bring a manservant running, at which point he addressed him in a low-pitched aside.

'You keep on disappearing like mist, *khriso mou*.' He inclined his handsome dark head in approval as one of the team of nannies hired to take care of the guests' children joined them and put out her arms to take Nicky.

'Oh, no...I'll take care of him,' Hilary said straight away.

'Nonsense. That is why the nannies are here, so that our guests can relax and enjoy our day with us,' Alexei pointed out lazily.

Billie passed over Nicky with pronounced reluctance. He began to complain but the nanny swept off again at speed and her son's muted cries of protest soon disappeared into the distance. Her cheeks pink, Billie gave Alexei a glance that spoke of reproach. With the cool intolerance of an autocrat, he had banished Nicky from their wedding celebration for the simple sin of crying. She folded her empty arms, shaken by how protective she felt of her child and of how much she longed for the nerve to chase after the nanny and retrieve him. Alexei had to be told the truth about Nicky's origins soon…he *had* to be!

'You shouldn't have interfered,' Billie remarked as her aunt drifted off at a signal from her sister—Billie's mother, Lauren.

'As a good hostess you should have taken care of the problem for your aunt,' Alexei admonished smoothly. 'Hilary can't even dance with a baby in tow. I should imagine she'll be glad of a break from the incessant demands of so young a child.'

At that rebuke, the colour drained from Billie's face, leaving her pale while her soft brown curling lashes screened her discomfited gaze. She was shaken by the awareness that Alexei had spoken the truth and that it was a truth that she had ignored in her eagerness to keep her son within reach. Nicky should have been passed over to the nanny team earlier in the day along with all the other young children, leaving her aunt free to take full relaxed advantage of a rare day out. More and more she was appreciating just how complex and challenging her deception had become. She was no longer being fair to Hilary. Although Hilary had agreed to look after her great-nephew and behave as though he were her son, neither woman had foreseen just how onerous and complicated that responsibility might become.

From the doorway, Billie regretted their combined naivety about Nicky while she watched as the captain of Alexei's yacht, Stuart McGregor, boldly swapped place cards at the top table to ensure that he got a seat beside her attractive blonde aunt. The older man had been keenly pursuing their acquaintance from the first day that he had met Hilary. He had already visited

Billie's house on several occasions, calling in on the pretext of books he wanted to loan her aunt and then inviting her out to lunch or for a walk. Although Stuart had yet to suggest that he was seeking anything more than platonic companionship from Hilary, the recent widow seemed to like Stuart and might well already be wishing that she could come clean and admit that Nicky was not actually her child. Billie realised that the pretence that Nicky was Hilary's son had put her aunt in a very awkward position. For the first time it occurred to Billie that a lot of people other than Alexei would condemn both women when the truth finally came out. After all, nobody liked to be lied to and deceived.

'You're very fond of Hilary's baby, aren't you?'

'Of course, I am,' Billie responded, almost wincing at the unnecessarily defensive note in her reply.

Alexei laughed softly. 'And the compliment is returned. The child was clinging to you with both hands like a little limpet.'

'The child's name is Nicky,' she told her bride-groom.

'Whatever.' Alexei had already lost interest in the topic and without further comment he curved an arm round his bride's slender body to direct her back into the airy room where their guests were already taking their seats for the meal.

The world-famous and very beautiful singer whom Alexei had engaged to entertain them while they ate rested her huge sultry brown eyes on the bridegroom and aimed every lovelorn pas-sionate note she sang in his direction. Steadily growing as rigid as a concrete post in her seat, Billie watched the byplay and registered that something much more important than good busi-ness was prompting the entertainer's behaviour. Evidently there was, or had been at one time, a much more intimate link between her husband and the artiste, the existence of which Billie had never suspected.

Before she could even think of what she should or should not say on that score, Billie found herself leaning closer to her new husband and

saying in an acid undertone new to her reper-
toire, 'You've slept with her, haven't you?'

Alexei quirked a satiric brow. 'I won't dignify
that question with an answer.'

'Well, it's pretty obvious to everybody here,'
Billie declared, refusing to heed the voice of caution chiming to be heard inside her head. 'I'd
have to be stupid not to see the way she's looking
at you.'

'I don't see a problem—'

'Well, I expect you wouldn't,' Billie agreed,
thinking bitterly that he was too accustomed
to receiving languishing looks and flirtatious
smiles from women to appreciate that his bride
might find such displays particularly offensive
on her wedding day. Just for once she would
have enjoyed the absence of that kind of bla-
tant behaviour in his radius. Just for once she
wanted to take pole position and shine more than
any other woman around him. As the juvenile
quality of her wishes pierced her, she almost
laughed. Since when had she wanted to show
off? And just when had she forgotten that she

owed the ring on her wedding finger to qualities that Alexei deemed superior to mere sexual attraction? It was a sobering acknowledgement.

'I don't expect you to fuss about such trivialities,' Alexei told her drily.

Billie bridled, as she very much disliked the suggestion that she had no right or excuse to experience feelings of resentment and disapproval when other women went out on a limb to give an unashamed sexual come-on to her new husband. Feverish colour highlighted her cheekbones and enhanced the bright emerald sparkle of her eyes. 'If it was an ex-lover of mine parading the fact in front of you, how would you feel?'

'I'd knock his teeth down his throat,' Alexei conceded with a softness that was all the more chilling for its assured cool and conviction. 'But then I'm the only lover you'll ever have, so, in our case, that situation will never arise. You're exclusively mine, *khriso mou*. I like and appreciate that.'

That macho response sent Billie's teeth flying together with a snap and she bit back a stinging response. It infuriated her that he was right, that he would never know the slightest discomfort on her behalf in another man's radius. She had no past, no sexual history to challenge his indefensibly sexist and hypocritical attitude, but then she *was* holding back on enough secrets to sink the *Titanic*, she reflected with a belated shiver of foreboding. It worried her even more that he was so confident that she was a virgin. It was a little too late to disabuse him of that notion now. She had allowed too many comments in that line to flow past her unchallenged. But after that night following the funeral when he had swept her off to bed with him, she was no longer intact. Would he be able to tell the difference? She very much hoped not.

She had already decided to wait until the next day before making a clean breast of events with regard to that night. She was praying that they could enjoy their wedding day and hopefully their wedding night as well without the daunting necessity of a confessional session that would shatter all harmony between them. Even

one night of intimacy would surely make Alexei
a little more understanding and approachable?
After all, nobody would be less tolerant than
Alexei when he suddenly discovered that he was
not in possession of all the information there was
to know about her, or indeed that she had gone
out of her way to conceal certain facts about
herself. Her troubled eyes resting on his hard
classic profile and the fundamental strength and
obduracy that were etched there, Billie struggled
to stay calm despite the daunting challenges that
lay ahead of her. With an idle thumb she massaged the new ring on her wedding finger as if
it were a talisman that would protect her.

'The only problem I can see right now *is*…your
mother,' Alexei delivered in a stern undertone.
'She's getting out of control.'

Billie's startled gaze followed his across the
room to where Lauren had risen from her seat
to begin dancing with a man, even though the
rest of the guests were still sitting. Her mother
cannoned clumsily into another table and then
a chair while continuing to laugh and talk very

loudly, all her attention predictably pinned to her male partner. Lauren, who had obviously imbibed a fair amount of alcohol, was impervious to the dirty looks she was attracting as those around her tried to concentrate on listening to the world-class performance the singer was putting on.

'Oh, for goodness' sake!' Billie framed between gritted teeth because she was mortified by her mother's rude behaviour. A thousand times and more, when she was younger, Billie had suffered similar squirming moments when her parent made a spectacle of herself in public. But today of all days was special! Already very conscious of her humble beginnings, Billie had prayed beforehand that, just this once, Lauren would not embarrass her by doing anything to draw attention to herself in polite company. But her mother, it seemed, would always be as irresponsible as a defiant teenager, particularly if there was an attractive man within her radius. In the background Billie saw Hilary rise from the same table and advance on her giggling, swaying sister.

Lauren paid heed to Hilary in a way she wouldn't have to her daughter. Within the space of a minute the dancing display was over. Lauren returned sulkily to her seat while the man she had been dancing with returned to his at an adjoining table.

'Thank goodness for Hilary,' Billie remarked with relief. 'Who's the man that Lauren was with?'

'One of my cousins, who is old enough to know better.'

'Age doesn't necessarily make people wiser,' Billie retorted half quietly; the supposed wisdom of experience and maturity had made little mark on Lauren, who remained as giddy as an adolescent. What was more, Billie thought ruefully, men always seemed to quickly shed their inhibitions and behave badly in her mother's company.

'Don't make yourself responsible for Lauren any more,' Alexei urged Billie, surprising her with that unwelcome recommendation. 'She's not going to change. Just let her live her life.'

Billie thought that it was all very well for him to hand out such advice, but he had never had to cope with the hard reality of Lauren's problems when an affair broke up and she was abandoned once again. At such times, her mother would sink into depression and self-pity and use alcohol as a crutch and it was then that she needed her daughter or her sister. Without such support Lauren did not have the resources to pick herself up again.

'Of course, I will always support her financially,' Alexei added. 'You don't need to worry about that.'

Billie reddened. 'She's pretty much fine since I bought her the house. She doesn't need to hang on your sleeve—'

'I have plenty of relatives of my own who do,' Alexei fielded evenly. 'It makes sense.'

That Alexei was making a point of spelling out his intentions towards her feckless parent surprised Billie and made her smell a rat. 'What do you know that I don't know?' she prompted, wondering if her mother had got into financial trouble again and if it was possible that Lauren had made a direct request to him for his help.

'I don't want to talk about this now,' Alexei answered coolly.

And Billie found herself thinking of all the many occasions when, as an employee, she had had no choice but to respect such arrogant embargos. 'She's my mother. I have a right to know what's going on.'

Alexei dealt her a dark look of exasperation. 'Do we really have to discuss your mother's debts on our wedding day?'

Hot colour ran up like a banner below Billie's fair skin and her slender spine stiffened. It was news to her that Lauren had run up debts again and she was furiously embarrassed by the revelation. 'You should've told me—'

'Why?' Alexei sent her an impatient glance. 'Your problems are my problems now.'

With effort Billie overcame the sense of humiliation that was threatening to overpower her. She grasped that he'd had no prior intention of telling her and regretted her own persistence.

'Just one more question—how did you find out that Lauren had such problems?'

'Speros is a small place.'

That revealing assurance ensured that Billie's sense of mortification and shame lingered. The awareness that some islander, probably either a tradesman or a shopkeeper, had clearly approached Alexei on the score of an unsettled bill cut her to the quick. For years she had been proud of the fact that the financial help she'd given her mother had prevented such embarrassing situations from arising. She remembered too well how it had felt as a child when Lauren had owed money everywhere in the village.

'It's time for us to dance,' Alexei breathed, closing a hand over Billie's and raising her from her seat.

Unmercifully conscious of being the cynosure of attention when she was much more accustomed to playing the role of a backroom girl, Billie found it impossible to lean into the strong, hard support of his tall muscular length. Lean fingers splayed across the curve of her hips and sexual heat flared through her in jagged response.

'Why are you so tense?' Alexei censured in a roughened undertone. 'You feel like a little steel girder in my arms.'

Billie had to force her slender body to yield into his. She was quivering with tension and the sudden onslaught of a sexual awareness that was almost painfully strong. Memories of their short-lived intimacy on the night that Nicky was conceived were sizzling through her and her body was awakening again, shedding the taut suppression of feelings and tight self-discipline that she had practised for so many months.

'That's better, *khriso mou*,' Alexei told her thickly, shifting against her so that even through the barrier of their clothing she could feel the unmistakable urgency of his arousal.

And a kind of heavenly satisfaction enveloped Billie at that instant, for she had never truly managed to see herself as a sexually appealing woman in Alexei's eyes. After all, what they once briefly shared had been unreservedly forgotten by him and she had found it hard to equate that cruel hard fact with the idea that their intimacy had been in any way special on his terms. But now, in the most primitive way of all, she could enjoy the proof that Alexei wanted her as a man wanted a woman and as a husband wanted a wife. *Her*, miraculously; not one of the more beautiful and sophisticated women present who had entertained him most successfully, though if only for a little while. And what if she came to the same end? The thought struck like a dagger in Billie's vulnerable heart. What if those gossiping exes of his were right and Alexei got bored and swiftly realised that he had made a mistake in marrying her?

Anxious green eyes screened, she luxuriated in his embrace while her mind teemed with rampant, fearful thoughts that dismayed her. Since when had she been so scared? But all too often in recent months Billie had appreciated that loving Alexei and having Nicky had changed her in a fundamental way: she was much more at the mercy of her emotions than she had once been.

And, of course, she was nervous about the future. After all, Alexei wasn't in love with her. He had married her on the rebound after breaking off his relationship with Calisto Bethune. That particular taunt, overheard in the cloakroom, had not been without foundation. Alexei had chosen Billie as a wife because he believed he knew her well and considered her to be thoroughly sensible and trustworthy. He had *not* chosen her because she was gorgeous, exciting or fantastic fun. He had picked her with his head, not his heart, deeming her perfect for the role of a conservative, low-maintenance wife. How would he react tomorrow when her revelations forced him to appreciate that she was as flawed and imperfect as any other woman?

They left the floor to circulate among their guests. Later, in the early evening, Hilary, her eyes full of dismay, sped over to her niece and whispered urgently, 'Lauren's talking in the room next door. She's drunk and saying silly stuff. She wouldn't listen to me—'

'I'll come with you.' Sliding free of Alexei's hold, Billie hurried in her aunt's wake.

Lauren was easily spotted. The table in front of her was littered with empty glasses. With a cigarette in one hand and another burning in the ashtray beside her, Lauren was revelling in being the centre of attention.

'Billie!' Lauren exclaimed with enthusiasm when she laid eyes on her diminutive daughter. 'You know that's not her actual name. That's what Alexei christened her when she was a kid— her real name is Bliss…'

'What else can you tell us, Lauren?' an eager brunette prompted.

'Obviously, I know where all the bodies are buried!' Throwing back her shoulders in emphasis and exposing rather too much bosom in her low-cut dress as she did so, Lauren widened suggestive eyes, only to start coughing violently as the smoke from her cigarette wafted up into her face.

'There are no bodies,' Billie interposed firmly,

finding her way to the bedraggled blonde's side and slapping her on the back.

'Don't listen to her…there's lots of bodies!' Lauren carolled rebelliously loudly. 'And one of them is very little. In fact, I warned my daughter to keep all her secrets until she was safely married. At least that way even if the marriage crashes and burns, she'll be rich and secure—'

Losing all patience in the wake of that outburst, Hilary grasped one of her sister's arms and hauled her bodily from her seat. 'It's time for us to go home now, Lauren—'

'I don't wanna go home,' the middle-aged blonde slurred as she swayed. 'I'm enjoying the party.'

A horrible little silence fell and only as she assisted her aunt with her stumbling, angrily muttering mother did Billie register that Alexei had joined them. Her face burning, her tummy twisting with fear, she clashed with blazing golden eyes.

'I've organised a car for you,' Alexei told Hilary in a gentle undertone as a nanny appeared to pass over Nicky into her care. 'I'm sorry that you have to leave early.'

Lauren, who, for all her outspokenness, was intimidated by her son-in-law, had turned an ashen colour and was now avoiding both his gaze and her daughter's. Billie was wan and uncomfortable as she watched her aunt leave with Nicky and her mother.

'I think Lauren may well need professional help,' Alexei breathed with icy cool.

'Sorry. I know she's an embarrassment…but professional help?' Billie echoed, finally working up the courage to look directly at him.

'A stint in rehab might at least cure her of looking forward to our marriage crashing and burning,' Alexei countered sardonically, brilliant golden eyes cutting as lasers. 'Clearly she hasn't read the terms of our pre-nup. But what the hell was she talking about? Buried bodies? *Secrets?*'

Pale as milk, Billie trembled as she registered how close her mother had come to exposing Nicky's parentage in public. 'She was drunk and getting carried away with all the attention she was getting—that's all. But I don't think she needs to be packed off to rehab just yet—'

'Leave me to deal with Lauren,' Alexei interrupted with ruthless cool. 'I understand her better than you do.'

And Billie, accustomed to her mother's single-minded obstinate egotism, reckoned that he very probably did.

CHAPTER TWO

IT WAS after midnight. The bride and groom had stayed with their guests until late, then had then taken a motor launch out to Alexei's yacht, *Sea Queen*. But lights in Billie's own little house were still twinkling brightly back on shore, Billie registered as she stood on the private deck beyond the incredible luxury of the stateroom suite. Hilary, at the very least, was still awake. Was Lauren still with her sister and behaving badly? Or was Nicky reacting poorly to his disrupted routine and preventing her aunt from getting the rest she needed? Billie's arms felt horribly empty. Her heart ached at once again having to face the prospect of leaving her infant son.

Only for a week, though, Alexei had sworn. He was no big fan of honeymoons or indeed any enforced break from business, but he was also too astute not to recognise that to neglect any show of intimacy and togetherness after their wedding would attract the kind of comment that might embarrass his bride. And tomorrow Alexei would finally know everything there was to know about her, Billie reminded herself doggedly. The pretences, the lies would mercifully end there. There would be no more secrets. He would understand her attachment to Nicky, but how would he feel about suddenly and without any preparation at all becoming a father?

Billie shivered in the cool crisp late spring air. A light step sounded behind her and Alexei closed his arms round her from behind, drawing her back into the heat and shelter of his tall, muscular body. 'That was one very long day,' he sighed above her head. 'How the hell did my father manage to go through with marrying four times over?'

'I suppose the fact that he kept on trying to find the right wife says a lot about his optimistic outlook,' Billie remarked, her voice wavering as her bridegroom pressed his mouth sensually to the tender skin where her shoulder met her neck. She was not aware that it was a sensitive spot, but it sparked a surprising burst of heat low in her pelvis and she trembled, straining back against him in response.

Alexei laughed softly. 'Don't be so naïve. He only married my mother because she was carrying me. He wanted a son and heir more than he ever wanted any woman—'

Cooler air brushed Billie's spine while he unhooked the back of her gown with the lazy pace of a gourmet contemplating a six-course banquet. 'You're so cynical!' she returned.

'The marriage might have been a success on your terms, but even my mother knew that he would never have married her had she not conceived. She was a nobody from nowhere…'

'Like me,' Billie could not resist commenting in receipt of that arrogant opinion.

'No. You're a local girl with a clever brain and a colourful background,' Alexei teased, sliding his hands below the loosened bodice of her dress to find the firm thrusting softness of her breasts. 'And now you're my wife, my perfect wife, *khriso mou.*'

Her breath caught in her throat as he expertly massaged her swelling nipples between thumb and forefinger, sending sharp arrows of desire darting to the very centre of her restive body. Helpless in the grip of those sensations, she leant back against him and he swept her up into his arms and carried her back into the stateroom. Setting her down he peeled her out of the gown he had undone and lifted her clear of the foaming swathe of petticoats.

'Full marks for surprising me,' Alexei quipped, pausing to take in the full effect of her turquoise satin and lace lingerie and the lacy hold-up stockings she sported on her slim legs.

Although rosy colour warmed Billie's face beneath his lingering appraisal and her breasts shimmied in the turquoise satin cups as her breathing increased in rapidity, she countered, 'I'm a bride…what did you expect?'

'White cotton, no frills,' he told her frankly,

resting her down across his long powerful thighs while one strong arm supported her spine.

Billie gazed up into brilliant golden eyes and her heart felt as if it were bouncing up onto a positive high of love. 'Oh, you'll see plenty of white cotton on the other three hundred and sixty four days of the year. This is a one-off,' she warned him deadpan. 'Enjoy it while you can.'

And Alexei laughed and kissed her, framing her face with spread fingers, delving into the moist tender interior she offered long and deep until her heart was thumping like a piston and she was kissing him back hard, revelling in the wicked pleasure of being crushed against him. He released the catch on her bra and moulded the lush fullness of a rose-tipped mound with reverent appreciation. 'You can have no idea how many times I've fantasised about your breasts...'

'In the office?' Billie gasped, taken aback by that candid admission.

'You look so shocked.' Alexei was laughing

again, both hands now fully engaged in massaging the swelling bounty of her creamy flesh.

'Well, it's not very professional, is it?' Billie complained, embarrassed for herself in the past.

'But I only looked and imagined. I didn't touch,' he reminded her. '*Of course* I looked. I'm a man and the more you covered up, the more I noticed and wondered. Modesty is a great turn-on. If you'd sunbathed topless I'd have satisfied my curiosity long ago.'

As his skilled fingers found the distended tips of her nipples her eyes slid shut in an instant of intense arousal that made heat bloom like a yearning flower between her trembling thighs. But even as her body reacted she was thinking over what he said, registering that her discreet clothing and apparent reluctance had heightened his desire for her and immediately wondering whether constant marital availability would swiftly convert his interest to boredom. He bent her back over his arm and closed his mouth over first one throbbing reddened peak and then the other, laving her sensitised flesh with his tongue and grazing the beaded peaks with his strong white teeth. She gasped out loud, her body catching fire and flaming as fast and hotly as bone-dry straw. Rational thoughts fled her head like fallen leaves blown by the wind.

'I never thought I'd be so excited by my wedding night,' Alexei confided huskily, setting her aside and springing up to begin carelessly shedding his clothes. 'Congratulations, Billie. Experienced as I am, you make even sex feel fresh and new.'

Awesomely conscious of the stinging sensitivity of her nipples and the lush heat at the heart of her, Billie was dry-mouthed and all of a quiver, while wondering if she would ever be able to match his cool…or, for that matter, his evident expectations. So many women had tried and failed to hold his attention. Why should she be any different? Even to lie there half naked without rushing to cover up her exposed flesh was a challenge for Billie. Impervious to such insecurities, Alexei cast off his shirt, revealing the tightly

honed muscular magnificence of a torso sprin-
kled with dark whorls of hair, a narrow waist and
a stomach as flat as a rock slab. Physically he
was just pure perfection, she acknowledged, her
gaze riveted by his sheer spellbinding masculine
impact. He discarded his last garment and the
very boldness of his towering erection washed
colour over her face, for her memory—unlike
his—had no missing gaps and she was recalling
the velvet-sheathed-in-steel feel of him beneath
her fingers and moving inside her. Something
clenched deep in her stomach.

He lay down beside her and pulled her back
to him, crushing her mouth hungrily below his
with a hot sexual urgency that thrilled her. He
slid long fingers in a bold trail below her panties
and groaned with earthy satisfaction, 'You're so
wet and ready for me, *khriso mou.*'

Feverishly aware of that betraying damp heat,
she trembled beneath the confident touch of
his hand, raising her knees to assist him as he
skimmed off the final barrier between them. 'I
can't help wanting you,' she breathed shakily.

'And isn't that only as it should be?' Alexei husked, golden eyes glittering over her with virile approval even as his fingers came into contact with a roughness to the skin of her lower stomach that surprised him. 'What is this I feel?'

Billie froze, belatedly realising that he had found her Caesarean scar. 'Just a gynaecological thing—some surgery—I had,' she answered as casually as she could.

'You never mentioned it,' Alexei commented.

'Some things women like to keep to themselves.'

He shifted his hand back to a more sensitive spot and every skin cell in her quiveringly appreciative body seemed to leap. She was feeling too much to feel comfortable because her responses were already breaching the boundaries of her self-control. The exquisite pleasure of his skilled exploration of the slick folds of tender tissue between her thighs was almost more than she could stand without crying out aloud. She twisted and she turned until he stilled her and then she gritted her teeth together, her slender neck extending while he delicately teased the tiny erect bud of her clitoris and right then her concept of what was unbearable was rewritten from inside out. Her hips shifted and jerked upwards in a pleading motion and he lowered his dark arrogant head to the distended rigidity of her nipples, sucking them into his mouth and toying erotically with her wildly responsive flesh.

'Please...*please now*,' she framed brokenly, tormented by the burning heat of an excitement too much to be borne.

He came over her and into her in an almost simultaneous movement. With a sinuous shift of his hips he positioned his long powerful body and sank into her inner warmth with a low, melodious growl of sensual pleasure. For a split second, fear pierced the veil of her excitement and her inner muscles clenched hard round his swollen shaft. His golden eyes caught the momentary look of concern and unease she couldn't hide and then his hands closed round her hips and he drove into her again with hard, sure sensual force as if he knew the intensity of her need. The feeling of pressure low in her belly increased until all she was conscious of was the remorseless intrusion of his strong body into hers and the ravishing irresistible force of a physical stimulation so extreme it came close to pain. Tingling sparks of her impending release shot through her stomach and she writhed and gasped, her body arching as the most intense orgasm gripped her and sent wild sensation flooding through her in an uncontrollable and explosive tide.

The feeling of release from her earthly body was so powerful that for long moments after that climax Billie was in a daze. Only slowly did she regain awareness again, register the weightiness of her limbs, the heavy cocoon of sweet satisfaction that was reluctant to let her go, and even more slowly did she notice that Alexei had pulled away from her when she most wanted to cling to him. And then there was the silence… thrumming and taut as only a male as volatile as Alexei could make it. Her bright head swivelled on the pillow, green eyes very dark and wide flaring to Alexei.

He looked levelly back at her and a lump of dismay formed in her throat, for she read the challenge in his appraisal. The silence lay like a claustrophobic blanket threatening to stifle her ability to breathe. A whoosh of alarm ran down her spine like a cold warning hand. 'What's wrong?'

Thrusting the pillows back against the head-board, Alexei sat up. Brilliant golden eyes rested on her with all the extraordinary force of his fierce temperament. 'I'm amazed you have the nerve to ask me that. You lied to me, and you know how I feel about lies.'

Fear cut Billie as deep as a knife wound and a kind of panic raced like a wrecking ball through her more usually calm thoughts, creating mental havoc. Her blood ran cold, her skin turned clammy. *'L-lies?'* she queried, playing desperately for time.

'That certainly wasn't the very first time you had sex. You weren't a virgin before I married you, yet you were determined to make me believe that you were. What is that other than a lie?'

He was disappointed, she assumed, realising just what a pit she had dug for herself to fall into. How could she tell him the truth without telling him the *whole* truth? The few hours of grace she had believed she still had had suddenly vanished, depriving her of any control over the situation.

'Of course it would be downright hypocrisy for a guy of my experience to expect or demand a virgin bride in this day and age,' Alexei drawled in glancing continuance. 'I may have made a false assumption but you lied by omission. Lying by staying silent when you should have contradicted me is *still* a lie.'

'I didn't know how to tell you,' Billie framed uncertainly. 'When you made that assumption I felt trapped by it—'

'No, don't make the mistake of trying to lay your dishonesty at my door,' Alexei cautioned her, his lean handsome face hardening into grim lines at her response. 'I also want to know who

your first lover was: Damon Marios, your spine-
less first love?'

The instant he flung that arrogant demand and
that name at her she froze, wondering whether
she really had to trail out all her secrets there and
then, if there was no escape, no other way of de-
flecting him. And then she marvelled at her own
reluctance to speak, her terror of breaking free of
the cosy bridal bubble of happy-ever-afters and
fantasy. 'You're not going to believe me when I
do tell you who it was.'

As he stared at her from below the dense dark
screen of his luxuriant lashes Alexei's handsome
mouth took on a sardonic quirk. 'Try me. At
least you have the wit not to persist in the lie.'

Billie no longer felt comfortable in the bed.
She was no more comfortable under his intent
scrutiny when she slid out naked from below
the sheet to move a few steps away and reach
for the light silk robe draped in readiness for
her use over a chair. Enveloped within its con-
cealing folds, the sash tightened round her waist

with unsteady hands, she felt curiously more in control again.

'How did you know? How did you guess?' she suddenly pressed, unable to resist asking that question.

'You told me. You betrayed yourself by the expression in your eyes, your face, your very responses. You looked and acted guilty.'

'Because that's how I feel and it's really not fair because not all of this is my fault,' Billie reasoned with a defensive edge of defiance. 'You can't be so judgemental about lies. Not everything is that black and white.'

'Spare me the moral philosophy speech,' Alexei derided. 'You may be my wife but one thing hasn't changed: I still expect a straight answer to a direct question.'

'You asked me who my first lover was but, quite honestly, you have no right to ask me that question!' Billie dared, flashing that answer back to him in retribution.

Alexei dealt her an arrested appraisal, her insubordination clearly coming as an unwelcome surprise to him.

Billie was trembling. 'I mean, how do you even dare to ask me that question?'

His golden gaze was splinteringly hard and unyielding. 'I dare because you're my wife and nothing in your life should be hidden from me.'

Billie tried and failed to swallow at that bold, startlingly idealistic expectation. A tiny pulse at the base of her throat was flickering wildly. The tip of her tongue snaked out to moisten the taut dryness of her full lower lip. '*You* were my first lover…but you don't remember the time we spent together—'

His ebony brows drew together. 'What the hell kind of nonsensical claim is that?' Alexei demanded, his raw impatience unhidden.

'It may sound like nonsense to you at this moment, but it's still the truth. On the night of your parents' funeral, when everyone else had gone home, you had been drinking and you went to bed with me,' Billie recounted, her agitated fingers knotting into the too long sleeves of her robe and tugging in a restive motion at the cuffs.

'Any moment now you'll be telling me that you were abducted by aliens! Are you crazy?' Alexei jibed, tossing back the bedding and springing from the bed, a tall, powerful figure all the more daunting unclad. 'Or are you drunk? That's the only explanation I can come up with!'

'We made love in the guest suite where I was staying at the time. We had no contraception. You were heading back to your own room for condoms when you tripped and fell down the steps by the swimming pool. When you came round, you didn't remember that you'd been with me…' Billie's taut voice quivered with tension as he came to a halt, wheeled round and stared at her with frowning questioning force: she had finally won his full attention. 'You thought you'd been in the swimming pool because your hair was damp but you'd only been in the shower…'

Dark eyes blazing wrathful gold, he studied her, his lean, strong visage clenched into forbidding lines. 'No, Billie,' he cut in icily. 'You're very ingenious but I won't fall for a story like that. You tell me that we slept together on the one night of my life that I can't fully recall and you expect me to believe you? How stupid do you think I am?'

In a growing state of confusion, Billie gazed back at him. She had known it would be a challenge to make him believe her, but it had not crossed her mind that he might suspect her of fitting fictional facts to an actual event to provide back-up for what he deemed to be lies. 'But we really *were* together that night.'

'So, according to you, unlike every other woman I have ever met, you gave me your body and expected nothing in return—not even an acknowledgement from me?' Alexei slashed back at her with incredulous scorn. 'At least come up with lies that make some sense!'

Anger licked like a hungry flame out of her bone-deep anxiety. She felt as if she were fighting for her life and certainly for the love of it. Not so very long ago they had enjoyed an instant of perfect harmony out on deck and she had been so happy. 'When have I ever lied to you?' she queried emotively.

'What about those weeks before our wedding when you were playing the innocent little virgin charade? You need to fine-tune those principles I mistakenly thought you had. It's not the lie you allowed to stand, it's the fact that you were dishonest that disgusts me.'

Every word Alexei spoke flailing her like a whip, Billie had lost colour. Her body, so lately hot and damp from the vigour of his lovemaking, suddenly felt cold and shivery. Her green eyes dominated her heart-shaped face but the anger that had awakened inside her was already climbing higher and growing stronger in her defence. How dared he say that she disgusted him after all she had gone through on his behalf? She had stood by in silence while he romanced Calisto and slept with her. She had endured her pregnancy and the birth of his child without his support. *How dared he judge her?*

'Don't you dare tell me that I disgust you!'

Hard-as-granite dark golden eyes raked over her slight figure before finally condescending to meet her incensed gaze. 'It's the truth and that's all I've ever wanted or expected from you: the truth,' he told her insistently. 'If you can't even give me that, what have we got?'

That harsh question assailed her like water dripping incessantly on stone, for no matter what excuses she gave and no matter what words she spouted she would still be faced with the reality that she had lied to him. And just then, as he stepped into the shower and switched on the controls, Alexei was a formidable presence, terrifyingly immovable in his stubborn conviction. Rigid with tension, she went back into the stateroom. She quailed at the prospect of telling him about Nicky right there and then. If he couldn't even credit her claim that he had once made love to her, how likely was it that he would accept that he was the father of the child he didn't yet know she'd had?

Her slender hands clenched into fists as she attempted to will greater strength into herself.

Hilary had insisted that her niece should tell Alexei the truth before the wedding, and Hilary had been right, Billie acknowledged with fierce regret over her own weakness. Instead of respecting the sound ethical base of her aunt's argument, Billie had listened to Lauren, her self-serving and avaricious mother, who had never let notions of what was right and decent come between her and anything that she wanted. Billie had wanted that wedding ring at any cost, and now that she had it on her finger it felt like an own goal, a mockery, an empty promise...*why*? They had only been married for a matter of a few hours and Alexei had just told her that she disgusted him.

Billie sat down on the richly upholstered chair and surveyed her extravagant surroundings with blank eyes. Although it was warm, she felt cold. Shock was setting in and hitting her hard. He was the guy that she loved and she had burned her boats so thoroughly that she did not know how to go back and retrace her steps. Just then, damage control seemed an impossibility. Nothing that she could say or do would alter the fact that she had lied. And in the same moment she recognised just how much falling in love and having a child had altered her, for she was so much more emotional than she had once been. That made her feel so vulnerable and she longed to slide back into the practical, less sensitive shell of the young woman she had once been.

Towelling his wet body roughly dry with impatient hands, Alexei listened to the silence from the adjoining room. The silence only inflamed him more. He should have had the truth out of her by now, not those ridiculous lies! Discarding the towel, he strode into the communicating dressing room to pull out clothes. He was so angry that there was a tremor in his lean muscular hands. He stared down at them with brooding dark eyes and clenched his teeth together hard. Billie, whom he had trusted. *Ise Vlakas!* Stupid, he called himself angrily. Why had he placed such faith in her when he had long known that precious few women could be trusted? He had long accepted that many women would do virtually anything to get close to a man as hugely wealthy as he was. But that for her own ends Billie should attempt to make use of that particular night when he had drunk too much was an act of even more serious subterfuge and one that he considered unforgivable. To add more lies to the lies she had already allowed to stand between them was inexcusable. To think that he had thought her intelligent, worthy of being his wife, *perfect*….

Although in one sense, she had been perfect, Alexei conceded grudgingly as his mind roved back to their brief intimacy. A prickling heat at his groin and the stirring heaviness of renewed arousal assailed him while he recalled his bride's surprising wildness between the sheets. Her eager responsiveness and complete lack of control when he touched her had excited him—*she* had excited him more than any woman had in a long time. Any man would have rejoiced in receipt of such fervour. That passionate receptiveness had not been what he expected from a woman who was well known for her rigid self-discipline and old-fashioned notions.

Old-fashioned? His handsome mouth curled with renewed derision. What was truly real about Billie? And what was fake? Only hours earlier he would have sworn she was genuine one-hundred-carat gold, the real article, a woman he could actually respect...and *now*? He wondered if Damon Marios had taken her virginity, or whether it had been one of his other employees, or even whether the identity of Billie's secret lover lay far back in her youth. But why should the man's identity even matter to him? He had never been a possessive man, particularly when it came to sex. He was too practical to be otherwise. The crux of the matter was that Billie had lied.

Distaste filling him afresh, Alexei strode out of the dressing room, across the spacious stateroom and out of it again without even acknowledging her presence. He would give Billie time to consider her options before he left *Sea Queen*.

He was already considering his own: he had no intention of staying married to a woman he couldn't trust.

CHAPTER THREE

FRESH from the shower, Billie tackled her tangled and damp hair until it dried in a heavy silken swathe across her shoulders. She breathed in deep and set off to find Alexei. She was not a coward, she had *never* been a coward; he would listen to her, he *had* to listen to her. That was the only hope of salvation that she had left. Yet she knew how hard Alexei Drakos could be, how uncompromising, how very cold-blooded when his own interests were at stake...

Alexei was working at his laptop in the office just as if it were the middle of his working day rather than halfway through his wedding night. His luxuriant blue-black hair gleamed below the discreet down-lighters, lush dark lashes casting crescent shadows across his exotically high cheekbones. It was a pose she had seen him in a thousand times before and she had known exactly where to find him—at times of stress, Alexei always took refuge in work. But she could read the tension still etched into the lineaments of his classic profile and the warning flare of his straight aquiline nose as he lifted his proud dark head and saw her in the doorway and his grim golden eyes hardened.

'I know you're angry with me but I have to talk to you,' Billie said with low pitched urgency. 'I have to tell you what I've done—'

'What you've *done*?' Alexei repeated drily, a slanting brow quirking in emphasis. 'Does this relate to Lauren's loaded comments about knowing where the bodies are buried?'

That was a question that Billie would have preferred not to have to answer just then. But the awareness that she could not afford to play with the truth even just a little froze her in place. Slowly she nodded in reluctant affirmation of that point and watched his lean strong face darken in angry acknowledgement.

'Even your mother knows what I do not?' Alexei demanded.

'Yes. I did try to keep it all private but I'm afraid she worked out what I didn't tell her for herself,' Billie confessed quietly.

Alexei let his gaze roam over her small straight figure. For once what she wore enhanced rather than concealed her body and it was obvious that she was naked below her robe. The lush curves of her breasts were clearly delineated by the thinly draped silk and the tip-tilted swollen nipples that had thrilled to his attention were still tantalisingly prominent below the fine material. The heaviness stirring at his groin forced him to shift position in his seat while he wondered cynically if that revealing wrap had been chosen purely for his benefit.

Regardless of that suspicion, desire slivered through him and the strength of his sudden heated arousal took him aback. Just for once, satisfaction had not led to satiation. But then the very force of what he was feeling, that pungent mass of anger, bitterness and disillusionment, required a physical response; he was far more comfortable with his body's natural appetites than he was with words or emotions. Determined to ease himself in the most effective way of all, he extended a lean hand to her in silence and with a wary look of surprise in her green eyes she was quick to grasp his fingers. Banding his arms round her slight length, he crushed her to his big powerful frame and claimed her soft mouth with hot, driving hunger.

'*Se thelo.*' Alexei told her bluntly that he wanted her in roughened Greek and as the heady combination of yearning and relief at that invitation gripped Billie it left her infinitely weak. His embrace had blown her vague expectations out of the water and with every erotic plunge of his tongue her legs felt more boneless and less able to provide independent support. So keen was she to bridge the gulf between them at that moment that he could have done virtually anything with her and she would have offered no objection.

With a bold tug on the sash of her robe so that the edges fell apart, Alexei lifted her up onto the desk. He moulded the lush, creamy swell of her breasts, tugging at her swollen nipples, before he lowered his dark head to close his mouth urgently to a pouting peak while he pushed her legs apart so that his fingers could slickly massage the tiny bud of her arousal and probe the excruciatingly tender pink flesh beneath. She whimpered, excitement shrieking through her in a great rampant roar of heat, her body eager for release from the terrible tension. That fast, she could think of nothing but the urgent craving that his skilful caresses had induced.

Her arms linked round his neck and she trembled as he settled his hands below her hips and pulled her closer to stand between her spread thighs. There was a split second when she was aware that he was donning protection and sanity almost came back to her but, an instant later, he drove his rigid shaft into her hot velvety depths and her slim body bucked and writhed in ecstatic response. He pushed her flat and raised her thighs to pound into her tight wet channel with ravishingly forceful thrusts. Sounds she couldn't control escaping from her throat, she was at the mercy of intense sensation and extraordinary pleasure. She was flung to a height and then the pressure and tightness in her pelvis broke and fireworks exploded inside her in a wild, jerking, totally uncontrolled release.

'*Efharisto*…thanks. That took the edge off my temper.' Alexei lifted her off the desk and deposited her in a bemused heap in a nearby armchair.

Blinking rapidly and still all of a quiver from the raw passion he had unleashed on her, Billie watched blankly as he strode into the washroom. She looked down at her naked breasts and, with a stifled exclamation of shock, reared upright to tie the robe securely closed again. That seeming necessity did, however, make her think of that well-known saying that talked of bolting the stable door after the horse had already bolted. She was so shocked by what had just happened between them that she was trembling.

She had not known that it was possible to make love like that, for everything to be so intense and wild that it overwhelmed every other thought and decent consideration. Nor had she ever suspected that she might have the capacity to enjoy such an encounter and that new knowledge shamed her in her own eyes. Indeed she was devastated by his demonstration of savage sexual power over her, because even though no such intimacies had even been on her mind he had taken her from cool passivity to the hottest orgasm without the slightest hesitation or difficulty. *That took the edge off my temper*, he had said, as if the taking of her body was on a par with a good gym workout. Her face burned scarlet at the recollection.

Across his desk as well, she recalled in consternation, mortified by the awareness that in spite of the chasm between them she had let him do exactly as he liked. Even so, it was still their wedding night, wasn't it? Saying no to her highly sexed husband would not be the wisest path to take if she wanted to heal the breach between them. And, of course, anything that could reduce the tension between them was sensible and good, she reasoned, raking her tangled hair back off her damp brow with an unsteady hand. After all, she still had to talk to him, but the prospect of doing so while her body still hummed, tingled and downright ached from the sexual *Blitzkrieg* of his was a major challenge.

Only the dark shadow of masculine stubble roughening his strong jaw line and sensual mouth marred Alexei's visual perfection when he rejoined her. His cream linen chinos and sweater were as expensive, tailored and sophisticated in style as any more formal wear. Black hair brushed back from his brow, Alexei looked startlingly handsome but worryingly untouched by the emotional vulnerability threatening her equilibrium. All over again she longed for the detachment and self-control she had once been able to call on around him, for it had protected her from pain.

'I believe you said that you had something to tell me,' Alexei drawled cool as ice, as if that episode of hot breathless sex had taken place only in her imagination.

Locking pained green eyes to his angular

bronzed face, Billie said quietly, 'You *were* with me on the night of your parents' funeral. After your fall I knew that you'd lost a couple of hours and were actually suffering from concussion, even possibly a form of amnesia, but I couldn't persuade you to seek medical help.'

Alexei straightened his broad shoulders, his imposing height of over six feet casting a long forceful shadow across the dimly lit room. His entire attitude was detached, even businesslike. 'I can't accept any part of your story. I would never have slept with you in such circumstances, and as for that tale you told about sex without contraception? I'm afraid that could only have happened in the fictional realms of your brain because, drunk or sober, I don't ever take risks in that line.'

In her eagerness to persuade him, Billie leant forward. 'I'm not lying and maybe you'll understand that better once I've told you everything—'

Dense ebony lashes screening his stunning eyes to a dangerous gleam of gold, his lean dark features were a mask of disdain. *'Everything?'* Alexei repeated with a saturnine look of mockery that sent the blood drumming heavily into her cheeks. 'What other strange fantasies have you dreamt up for my amusement?'

That piece of ridicule made Billie want to slap him hard. Her fingers clenched tightly together on that dangerous impulse. 'Maybe I was wrong not to tell you the truth months ago, but once you met Calisto the whole situation changed and I didn't feel I had any choices left. I assumed you were in love with her—you pretty much told me you were going to marry her. I had just discovered that I was pregnant. I was planning to tell you but you couldn't even remember sleeping with me—'

Black brows pleating together, Alexei cut boldly into that recitation. 'You were pregnant? By whom?'

Billie flung him a fevered glance of frustration. 'You're not that slow on the uptake—I conceived on the night of the funeral; I fell pregnant by you. You may not remember it but we made love twice without precautions.'

Alexei released his breath in a sharp exhalation, his instant dismissal of that possibility clear by his expression.

'Hilary's son is actually *my* son,' Billie spelt out, refusing to be daunted by that discouraging silence. 'He's my baby. I gave birth to him while I was on my career break in London. The only reason I asked for the leave was so that I could conceal my pregnancy.'

His brilliant eyes suddenly shimmered like a firework display, his outrage at what she was saying etched into every harshening angle of his lean darkly handsome features. 'Hilary's child is yours? You are telling me that you have actually given birth to a baby? That you deliberately concealed that fact from me and let me go ahead and make you my wife?' he roared at her in a sudden wrathful attack that made her shrink back momentarily into the shelter of her seat, shaken by his vehemence. 'And now you dare to try and pass off some other man's child as mine?'

Rigid with tension and with perspiration dampening her brow, Billie faced him. 'It's not like that at all. Nicky *is* your son. I've never been with another man.'

Alexei wasn't really listening. What he had learned was sufficient for him to make a judgement. A red mist of rage was burning through his brain while he struggled to put together what she had told him. His bride was a mother…she had a *child*? Appalled by that revelation, he remembered the seam of scar tissue low on her abdomen, which only hours earlier she had passed off as 'a gynaecological thing'. A Caesarean scar, he guessed, for the first time seeing a solid foundation to what had initially struck him as incredible claims. He could not at first get over his sense of shock that she could have concealed so much from him and even the most cursory appraisal of the past year or so warned him that Billie must have spun him an elaborate ongoing pack of lies in an outrageous attempt to pass off her child as his. Of course, she was anything but stupid. She knew that that was the only circumstance that might give her the hope that he wouldn't divorce her.

Golden eyes steadily chilling to the temperature of a sunlit iceberg, Alexei surveyed her. 'What a devious little schemer you are! You have the nerve to sit there looking me in the eye while you confess that you lied and cheated your way to the altar knowing that I would never have married you had I known the truth about you!'

Billie leapt up, her long, thick, wine-red hair rippling like bright ribbons across her shoulders and sliding across her cheekbones to highlight her pallor. 'That's not how it was, Alexei. There were lies and I'm sorry for that, but there was no cheating. Nicky is your son. How was I supposed to persuade you of that fact when you couldn't even recall being with me?'

'I assume you have heard of DNA testing?'

Hotspots of pink deepened the hue of Billie's cheeks in reaction to that unexpected taunt.

'This kid is…what age?' Alexei queried.

'He's four and a half months old. But when he was born you were still with Calisto and thinking about marrying her,' Billie referred to his ex-girlfriend, Calisto Bethune, with a heavy heart. 'I didn't want to cause trouble. I saw no benefit to anyone in doing that. It seemed to me,' she continued painfully, 'that you didn't want to remember being with me, and that probably everyone concerned would be happier if that night remained a secret.'

'I don't believe for one moment that your child is mine,' Alexei declared with icy conviction. 'I refuse to believe it. I hope you don't plan to take these insane stories into court with you. You will make a laughing stock of yourself—'

'Into…court?' Billie echoed shakily. 'What are you talking about?'

'Do I really need to spell out the fact that what you've just told me is grounds for divorce?'

Billie turned as cold as though he had just plunged her into an ice bath, consternation and shock gripping her hard. 'I know that you're shocked by what I've told you—'

'Of course I'm shocked by the image of you, your mother and your aunt plotting against me like Macbeth's three witches! 'Alexei derided with ferocious bite.

Billie's temper flared and she flew upright. 'It's ridiculous to talk like that. Nobody *plotted* against you! When I persuaded Hilary to pretend that Nicky was her child, my only motivation in doing so was to hide Nicky's parentage and protect you.'

'*You* wanted to protect *me*? 'Alexei exclaimed harshly, his contempt for that claim unconcealed. 'Even now in the midst of your attempt to palm off your bastard child on me, you can't tell me the truth! My proposal of marriage was what motivated your lies and deception—'

'How could it have been?' Billie flung back fierily, standing her ground to challenge him. 'My pretence that Nicky was my aunt's child began when I first told you that she was pregnant and asked for a career break. And that was months before you even considered marrying me!'

Stumped by that inescapable fact, Alexei

studied her with enraged hauteur, his glittering gaze bright against his superb bone structure. 'You lied to me and you deceived me over a very long period—'

'But not with any malicious intent!' Billie rushed to interpose, desperation racking her with a level of fear that did nothing to clarify her state of mind. 'I admit that I should have told you about Nicky before the wedding but I didn't have the guts—'

'Naturally avarice and ambition won out over honesty. Why? Only because you knew there would be no wedding if you told me the truth about yourself.'

'The very last thing I have ever wanted from you is money!' Billie launched back at him, angrily objecting to that base accusation. 'And don't refer to my son as a bastard ever again. However he was born, whoever he is, I love him and I'm proud of him. If you think so badly of me, how could you make love to me again?'

That emotive demand made Alexei's jaw square and he sent her a flashing look of scorn. 'That was just sex, a primitive urge for physical release, nothing more complex.'

Her face flamed and then slowly paled as his response sank in and trampled her pride into the dust. She wished with all her heart that she had said no, pushed him away, stuck to the business of confession and blame. But what was done was done and she could not change it. In spite of that sophisticated façade, Alexei had a primal streak that ran through him like tempered steel and powered his volatility and his ruthless-ness. He was a Drakos through and through. His father, Constantine had not hesitated to di-vorce the blameless third wife who'd adored him, and replace her with his pregnant mistress. Alexei, it seemed, would be equally quick to discard her now that she had disappointed his expectations.

'Nicky is your son,' she swore one last time, desperate to convince him of that crucial fact before he could tear their marriage apart.

'Nothing can excuse your lies and trickery,' Alexei drawled in a tone of finality. 'You cheated your way into our marriage and deserve nothing but my contempt. Naturally I'll order DNA tests, but only to ensure that you can't continue to allege that I fathered your baby.'

Humiliated by the threat of such testing being carried out on her child, Billie flung him a seething glance of condemnation. 'That's an insult! You're the only man I've ever slept with.'

Alexei rested forbidding dark golden eyes on her. 'I can't believe a word that comes out of your mouth and whose fault is that?'

He strode out of the room. Billie lingered in the shadowy office and struggled to cope with her unwieldy emotions. Their marriage had barely begun and she had wrecked it by keeping secrets from him, a little voice warned inside her aching head. She had lost his trust and it would not be easily regained. He was angry with her, very angry, but she had known he would be, she reminded herself dully. She heard the racket of rotor blades and unfroze to rush over to the desk and snatch up the phone. Captain McGregor informed her that Alexei had filed a flight plan for Monaco and had taken off in the helicopter with his security team. She thanked him for the information and replaced the receiver with a trembling hand and a heart racing like an overworked piston.

Alexei had just left her, walking out on her and their marriage. That realisation was a body blow that hit Billie very hard. She felt sick with the pain and trauma of that bold move and knew she had seriously underestimated his reaction to the secrets she had kept. It would be virtually impossible to influence a man who was determined to put an ocean between them. Few brides, however, were abandoned within hours of the wedding and Alexei's activities never passed under the media radar. The press would pick up the story of his unbridegroomlike behaviour and run with it for weeks.

Tears choking her and stinging her heavy eyes, Billie went back to the opulent stateroom in order to get dressed. It might not be dawn yet but the wedding night was well and truly over. She would take the motor launch back to

Speros and go home to look after Nicky. What else could she do? Her presence on *Sea Queen* had driven Alexei off his beloved yacht.

Was this it? Was their marriage over as well? Over even before it got past the beginning? She tried and failed to imagine Alexei giving her a second chance. Why would he do that when he had never loved her? Without love, what hold did she have over him? She had screwed up so badly that she hated herself at that moment. It seemed just then that keeping quiet about her pregnancy had cost her any hope of a happy future

CHAPTER FOUR

DURING the longest two weeks of her life, Billie followed Alexei's every move across the globe, for the pursuit of the paparazzi ensured that everything he did was reported in the tabloid press.

So, Billie got to know that Alexei stayed up two nights in succession at a Monaco casino gaming with a bunch of male friends. Then, after he went out to a fashionable nightclub in London she lay awake wondering whether, even though he had arrived and left alone, he had been with other women inside? Or indeed if at some more discreet location a woman had waited patiently for his visit. For the sake of her own sanity she tried not to read any more of the humiliating articles that speculated about the state and nature of the Drakos marriage.

All too many gossip columnists decided that Alexei had married his PA only because he would retain his sexual freedom with a wife who would appreciate her good fortune in marrying him too much to make unreasonable demands; a practical wife who didn't expect her gorgeous predatory tycoon to become as domesticated as a tabby cat. And, as another columnist quipped, Alexei Drakos was not the sort of guy likely to welcome rules. Alexei had always done what he wanted when he wanted without apology.

Old Drakos history was also dredged up, with Constantine's worst womanising exploits, even while married, spicily presented to entertain the readers even more. Billie felt doubly humiliated when far from flattering wedding photos of her, evidently taken with one of their guest's phones, appeared in print. Looking mousey and squat as she did in those horrible snaps she had felt that she was being shown up as the bride any self-respecting Greek tycoon and modern-day sex-symbol would desert.

'I just can't believe the way you're behaving!'

Lauren snapped with angry irritation, studying her daughter, who was playing with her son and Skye, the puppy. 'What were you thinking of when you moved back into this stupid little house? You're a Drakos now, you belong at the big swanky mansion next door! Of course people are talking when you're trying to act like the marriage never happened.'

Billie prevented the little black terrier from sinking her teeth into one of Nicky's toys, setting the item aside to be washed. 'I have no intention of moving Nicky into Alexei's house until he acknowledges that he is his son—'

'Oh, don't be more stupid than you can help!' Lauren hissed, her attractive face unattractively lined by her annoyance. As her shrill voice rose in volume the puppy fled behind the sofa. 'Leave the brat here with us and take possession of what's yours. You have the right to live in that villa—you're Alexei's wife!'

Billie glanced coolly at her mother. 'Don't call my son a brat!'

'You know I didn't mean it nastily,' her mother

argued. 'After all, Nicky—bless his little heart—is your golden goose. I mean, good grief, getting yourself pregnant was the only thing you did right! Alexei can do and say what he likes, but at the end of the day you will still be the mother of his son and heir and nothing can change that!'

'That kind of offensive talk isn't helping anyone, Lauren,' Hilary interposed, sending her a sister a reproachful look while she soothed and petted the puppy who had crept over to her feet. 'Billie is more interested in saving her marriage than in making a profit. I think she's right to stay here rather than up at the villa, particularly while Alexei believes that Nicky is not his child.'

At that moment, Nicky gave a chuckle of satisfaction. His big brown eyes looked up to his mother for approval and she told him what a beautiful boy he was. Anatalya, having firmly placed herself in Billie's support camp, arrived with the day's newspapers. While the housekeeper bent down to give Nicky her attention, Billie spread the papers across the dining table.

'You shouldn't look at them,' Hilary warned

her in the tone of a woman who knew her advice would be ignored. 'They twist the truth and print lies, and it upsets you.'

'I'm not upset and I won't get upset,' Billie vowed, only for the blood to drain from her features while she studied the latest photo of Alexei. There was no chance that what she was looking at was a lie, she reflected wretchedly. *If only it had been.* With a stunning lack of discretion for a married man, Alexei was seated at a fashionable pavement café on an elegant Parisian boulevard with a very beautiful blonde companion, a woman whom Billie had never expected to see in his company any more. 'Alexei's meeting up with Calisto again!' she cried strickenly before she could think better of that revealing outburst.

'I don't believe you,' Hilary breathed in disbelief, only to stare in dismay at the newspaper pages that her niece spread across her lap.

'I told you that you should have chased after him when he left the yacht,' Lauren sniped, staring over her sister's shoulder, unmoved by that shocking photo. It was obvious that her cynical expectations of her son-in-law had just been fully vindicated. 'Never let an angry man go if you want him back. Left to their own devices, they get up to all sorts of mischief!'

Billie was incapable of response. Just then, looking at Calisto with Alexei in Paris and thinking of them being together, she was living her every nightmare come true. Who had contacted whom first? Who had made that crucial first move? After being disillusioned by Billie, had Alexei turned straight back to the glamorous Greek divorcee for consolation? Was he already thinking that breaking off his relationship with Calisto had been a mistake?

A smart rata-tat-tat on the rarely used front door of her home made Billie jerk in surprise. 'Who on earth is that?' she muttered.

'I'll go and see.' Hilary was already out of her seat, keen to bury any further discussion about Alexei and Calisto Bethune in Paris. A minute later, however, Billie's attractive blonde aunt stuck her head back round the door and asked Billie to join her.

Billie was taken aback to find a trio of men standing in her hallway. Two of them were known to her and their appearance dismayed her a good deal: Baccus Klonis, the head of Alexei's legal team, and his second-in-command. Her face coloured with embarrassment. The third man was the doctor entrusted with the task of taking a DNA swab from the mouth of Nicky. Billie was stunned by their arrival without prior notice and the clear expectation that she would agree to the testing being carried out. While Hilary moved ahead of her to shepherd Anatalya, Lauren and the dog into the small seating area off the kitchen, Billie showed her visitors into the spacious lounge.

'Did Alexei ask you to do this?' she prompted tautly.

'Naturally I'm following Mr Drakos' instructions,' Baccus informed her with scrupulous politeness.

Billie felt as if she had just been slapped in the face and her cheeks reddened afresh. Even though Alexei might appear to be wandering

without purpose around Europe he had still contrived to consult his lawyers and it cut her even
deeper to learn that he had instructed them to
have their baby son DNA tested in spite of the
fact that he knew that Billie was against it. A
tense silence settled while Billie considered her
options. Of course she could withhold her consent to the test. Possibly Alexei even expected
her to refuse and he would undoubtedly consider a negative response as yet more evidence
that she was lying. It might be humiliating to
agree to her son being tested, Billie conceded
angrily, but at least it would prove his identity.
That at least would force Alexei to accept that
their intimate encounter had actually happened
somewhere other than in her imagination.

The doctor explained the simple procedure.
Billie scooped up Nicky. A swab was taken from
inside her child's mouth. Although it was ac-
complished in seconds and without causing her
child the slightest annoyance or discomfort, the
whole scene felt unreal to Billie and very much
like a nasty invasion of their privacy. Had she

and Alexei truly reached such an impasse that he had to treat her like this? And communicate with her only through his legal representatives? She watched the men leave and shivered as Hilary came up behind her and squeezed her taut shoulder in a quiet gesture of support and understanding.

'It had to be done,' her aunt said quietly. 'When Alexei realises that that little boy is his, everything is sure to change for the better.'

It was typical of Hilary to cherish an optimistic outlook. Billie was less confident. Was Alexei ready to be a father? She didn't think so. Would he begin to understand why she had behaved as she had? Or was she to be for ever condemned as a disgusting liar by a guy who had never had to adjust his black and white take on ethics for anyone's benefit?

'I think I'll go for a walk on the beach—'

'I'll put Nicky down for his nap,' Hilary cut in, well aware that her niece was eager to escape listening to what her mother would have to say about the DNA testing Nicky had just undergone.

A slender elegant figure in cropped brown trousers and a gold T-shirt, Billie paused at the roadside to allow a car to drive past. She gave a weak smile when the car stopped and Damon Marios lowered the window to greet her. 'I was just about to call on you—'

'I'm going down to the beach.'

With a nod as if she had issued an invitation, Damon parked his car on the broad verge and got out to join her.

'I don't think that us being seen together is likely to do either of us any good,' Billie remarked, secretly squirming with the anxiety over her marriage, which was urging her to exercise a rare kind of extreme caution. But when Alexei was being seen out and about with Calisto, what was she worrying about?

Damon cupped her elbow to steady her as she stumbled on her descent of the sloping ground that led down to the beach. 'Well, don't worry on my behalf. I'm getting a divorce…'

Billie turned dismayed eyes on him. 'But I thought you and Ilona were back together again.'

Damon released a rueful laugh. 'Yes, we were, but only briefly. I'm afraid the reconciliation didn't work out. Two years ago, Ilona fell for a colleague at work and had an affair and now that she's finally prepared to come clean on that score with her family and mine, we are both free to move on.'

Taken aback by that frank explanation, Billie spun and rested a sympathetic hand on his sleeve. 'I had no idea, Damon…I'm truly sorry.'

'It's most sad for our daughters. They don't understand why their mother is now bringing another man into their lives,' Damon replied heavily as he reached for her hand and squeezed her fingers. 'Ilona and I tried really hard to make a go of our marriage for their sake but we failed.'

Billie squeezed his arm. 'How are your family taking it?'

Damon rolled his eyes and grimaced. 'Like it's the end of the world, like nobody ever got a divorce before; like Ilona has suddenly become the most wicked woman on Speros.'

'I thought that was me!'

'Your husband's reputation goes before him. Everyone suspects Alexei of double-dealing.'

'In this case they would be wrong.'

'But not if the rumour that your aunt's child is in fact yours is actually true,' Damon chipped in, curious dark eyes settling on her flushed face.

'That is true,' Billie confirmed, since she had insisted that that deception was dropped the day after her wedding when she travelled back to the island alone. She could see that Damon was dying to ask who Nicky's father was and that only good manners were restraining him, but she dropped the subject. She had no intention of sharing her innermost secrets with the son of one of the biggest gossips in the village.

Forty-eight hours later, having stayed in London long enough to secure the purchase of several oil super-tankers at a fantastic price, Alexei flew home. The sun was going down over the island of his birth in a blaze of fire on the horizon. Full of all the splintering energy and impatience that characterised him, he sprang out of the helicopter and strode towards the villa whose many windows were reflecting the vivid skies. Most of his staff greeted him in the front hall. His keen gaze narrowed, for the one person he had expected to see was nowhere to be seen. He strolled down to the master suite to check out his suspicions and glanced into the dressing room. Thirty seconds later, he summoned Helios, his head of security, and asked a question. The answer he received infuriated him.

Billie was alone in her house when Alexei arrived. He walked straight through the back door, noting and disapproving of the fact that it was unlocked as it facilitated his entry. 'Billie?' he called out, frowning at the silence.

The kitchen was tidy, the living area empty. A black fluffy puppy peered out from behind a sofa at him, uttered a tiny tentative little bark and then hurriedly disappeared again, duty evidently done. Alexei's attention dwelt briefly on the basket of colourful toys and arrowed away again. Hearing music playing, he glanced into a bedroom and then noted the triangle of light showing to the side of the bathroom door, which had been left ajar.

Billie was enjoying a rare moment of self-indulgence and relaxation in the bath. Hilary had taken Nicky down to the village to see Lauren. She had not heard Alexei arrive because of the music and when the door opened she gasped in dismay and sat up in a sudden movement, water sloshing noisily round her. When Alexei appeared she was thunderstruck because he was the very last person she had expected to see.

Alexei focused on Billie in her sea of bubbles. Her creamy skin was wet and slick, the rounded globes of her rosy-tipped breasts invitingly pert and moist. His reaction to her was instantaneous; his body, which had been infuriatingly indifferent to the presence of other women, stirred into a rampant erection. Her generous pink mouth fell open on his name and, looking at the soft pink cushiony proportions of her lips, he knew for the first time in days exactly what he wanted and marvelled at the strength of his craving.

'Alexei...' Billie whispered unevenly, her bright head falling back and her green eyes widening to take in his tall muscular length with a sense of disbelief. His pearl-grey Italian suit had the sheen of silk and it hugged his broad shoulders, lean hips and long powerful thighs with the fidelity of the most expensive tailoring. Brilliant dark golden eyes gleaming from below the ebony screen of his luxuriant lashes, he looked spectacular enough to take her breath away.

'What the hell are you doing in here?' Alexei demanded in a wrathful undertone. 'Do you realise that I was able to just walk into this house? I could have been anyone...'

'You're probably the only person I know on the island who wouldn't bother to knock on the door and wait for an invitation,' Billie contradicted without hesitation.

'Where's your brain? I could have been a bloody paparazzo! Don't you realise how aggressive the press are now? You're not safe here without security. Get out of the bath,' he instructed her, extending a towel. 'I'm taking you home.'

'This *is* my home,' Billie protested, sitting firm and resolutely resisting a modest urge to cover her bare breasts, which she knew would provoke his scorn.

Alexei dealt her a splintering appraisal, his tough jaw line clenching at her defiance. 'You're my wife—you don't belong here any more.'

'You told me I was a disgusting liar and you walked out on our wedding night,' Billie reminded him tightly. 'I don't feel like your wife any more.'

'I've got the perfect cure for that.' Alexei strode forward and sank his hands below her arms. Before she could even work out what he was doing he had scooped her wet, resisting body out of the bath, set her down and enveloped her most efficiently in the folds of the towel.

'Stop it!' Billie shouted at him full throttle, trying to clumsily slap away his hands at the same time as she kept hold of the towel.

'If I walk out of here without you, I'm not coming back, *yineka mou*,' Alexei swore between clenched white teeth.

Billie froze as if an avalanche had suddenly engulfed her, stopping her in her tracks and depriving her lungs of oxygen. 'You can't threaten me like that!'

'It's not a threat, it's the truth,' Alexei countered harshly. 'Either you're with me, or you're not. I won't play games.'

In mute frustration, she watched him tug her wrap from the hook on the back of the door and extend it to her. He had the subtlety of an army tank on a battlefield. He had walked out on her and she longed to take a rebellious stance and defy his warning. But life just wasn't that simple, she acknowledged, digging damp arms into the sleeves of the wrap while letting her towel drop to her feet. She didn't know how to behave with him now, but he knew so well how to cut through all the aggravation to what really mattered. And what really mattered now was that she cared about him and loved him with all her heart, she reflected painfully. In his defence he was trying to bridge the gulf between them and their living in two separate houses would scupper any attempt to achieve that end.

'This isn't where you should be,' Alexei told her, his husky accent roughening his vowel sounds into a sexy growl as he backed her into the corner, wrenched the ties she was fiddling with from her grasp and knotted the sash with deft hands. 'You're coming home with me.'

And those words sounded so unexpectedly good to her that tears prickled at the backs of her aching eyes. The past fortnight of stress, gossip-column headlines and wild speculation had drained her strength and awakened her worst fears for the future. He contemplated her down-bent head and tipped up her chin so that he could see her triangular face again. The anxiety in her expressive eyes disturbed him but it didn't put a lid on the seething desire he was struggling to restrain. He had no idea why he wanted her so much at that moment. He only knew that her absence from his home where he had expected to find her had enraged and unsettled him to a degree that he was deeply uncomfortable with. Half-formed thoughts and jagged responses he didn't like were travelling through him, giving him an edgy and unfamiliar out-of-control sensation that he despised.

The atmosphere was so thick that Billie could taste it. He was frowning down at her, lean hands settling down on her shoulders with authority, the heat of him burning through the fine fabric of her wrap. She collided with scorching golden eyes and the quickening awareness low in her pelvis made her press her thighs together on the ache stirring between her legs. Uneasy with that piercing arrow of sheer wanton lust, she pulled away from him. 'I'll get dressed.'

'No.' Alexei closed a hand over her arm, pulling her back. 'There's no need. The car's outside. Someone will come over and pack for you.'

On the threshold of her bedroom, she stilled. 'What about Nicky?'

Alexei's big powerful body was resting lightly against hers, but when she posed that particular question he went rigid and his handsome dark visage set hard. 'He stays here.'

She twisted round, anguished eyes seeking his. 'I can't do that. He's my son, *my* responsibility.'

'You can visit…when I'm not around,' Alexei breathed with a raw note in his rich dark drawl. 'I'll cover his every need. He can have round-the-clock nannies, every luxury…'

'You can't ask me to choose between you!' Billie exclaimed wretchedly, suddenly grasping the devil's bargain he was laying down for her like a cruel gin-trap for the unwary foot.

Remorseless golden eyes struck her disbelieving gaze head-on. 'That's the deal for now and it's your choice.'

'I'm so sorry to interrupt,' another quiet familiar voice intervened and Hilary stepped into view in the living area, her face flushed with discomfiture. 'But you needed to know that you weren't alone any more. I'll take care of Nicky, Billie. You don't need to worry about him.'

Alexei thanked her aunt with grave courtesy

and Billie flung a questioning glance at the older woman, wondering why she was encouraging Alexei in his callous conviction that the obstacle of Nicky's very existence could be neatly set aside. And then it dawned on her that, within a few days at most, her son's paternity would no longer be in doubt. 'I don't want to leave him,' she admitted shakily.

'You and Alexei should have time alone as a couple. There's no harm in that,' Hilary murmured soothingly as if the situation were the most natural thing in the world.

Alexei directed Billie towards the back door as if the last definitive word had been spoken and was now etched in stone.

'I'm in my bare feet!' Billie objected jerkily.

'You don't need shoes!' Alexei countered, unwilling to countenance spending even five more minutes in what felt like the enemy camp. He bent down and swept her up off her feet into his arms.

'Please put me down,' Billie urged between

compressed lips while her aunt opened the door to smooth the progress of their departure.

Wearing a beaming smile, Helios stepped out of the huge black SUV outside to flip open the passenger door in readiness. Alexei stowed Billie into the rear seat and climbed in beside her. She gritted her teeth, horribly conscious of the reality that she was wearing neither make-up nor proper clothes. Impervious to any sense of awkwardness, however, Alexei made use of the brief drive to instruct Helios to organise a separate security team to watch over his wife.

'That's really not necessary,' Billie argued as the SUV swung up the driveway to the villa's imposing entrance.

'I know what's necessary,' Alexei asserted, settling a large domineering hand over hers where it rested on the seat. 'Whether you like it or not, you're at risk now as my wife and I want to know that you're safe, regardless of where you are.'

The presence of Helios and the driver made Billie restrain her snort of disagreement as she could not imagine what possible harm could come to her on Speros. Anatalya already had the front door open wide, and the housekeeper's eyes shone with satisfaction when she saw Billie inside the vehicle. Alexei scooped Billie out and strolled up the front steps into his home as if it were an everyday event to walk in carrying a wife clad in a dressing gown. He had always had that kind of ultimate cool, even as a boy, she recalled, and a sharp little pain stabbed through her as she thought of all that she stood to lose if their marriage broke down. Oddly enough, until that moment it had not occurred to her how deeply embedded Alexei was within even her life memories. Pausing only to instruct Anatalya to have Billie's clothes removed from her home and ask when dinner would be ready, Alexei took Billie into the master bedroom suite.

Billie sucked in a steadying breath as Alexei set her down on the carpet. 'We can't just act like these past two weeks never happened.'

Alexei swung round, his keen dark gaze grim. 'For the moment, why not? Of course, you could cut a lot of the **** out of this by just telling me the truth now. I would rate you higher for that than if you force me to drag the truth out of you *after* the DNA-test results.'

With a rueful sigh, Billie sank down on the side of the stylish big bed. 'It would have been easier if you had just left me where I was for now. Why did you insist on bringing me back here tonight?'

Doffing his jacket and wrenching off his tie, Alexei sent her a darkling glance of warning as though she had strayed into a conversational no-go area. Muscles rippling through the fine silk of his shirt, he bent to remove his shoes. 'I want a shower before dinner...'

Billie tried to avoid the temptation of watching him undress, but she learned that she hungered for even that small intimacy. Black hair tousled, strong jaw shadowed by blue-black stubble, he was stripping off his clothes without a hint of self-consciousness. 'I've nothing to wear here,' she pointed out. 'I left half my clothes on *Sea Queen*.'

Alexei laughed. 'I would be quite happy for you to dine with me naked.'

'It's not going to happen.' Billie knotted her hands together and watched him lift the house phone by the bed to issue a command and then discard his shirt and shoes. Every lithe movement of his lean bronzed body mesmerised her: he was utterly gorgeous. A knock sounded on the door and he strode over to answer it and accept the garment bag and boxes he was handed. He dumped them on the bed.

'That's the clothing problem solved,' he said with distinct satisfaction.

'These are for me?' Astonished, Billie unzipped the garment bag and pulled out a flamboyant, strappy scarlet dress. 'You bought this for me? But when?'

'I saw it in a window in Paris. You wear drab colours. I thought that I would enjoy seeing you in something bright for a change.'

Once again, Alexei had contrived to confound her expectations. He might have met up with Calisto in Paris, but while he'd been there he had also contrived to go shopping on his wife's behalf. She pulled open the other packages and her complexion warmed when she saw the zingy red lingerie and high heels, which carried a much more sexual message.

'Those items were pure self-indulgence,' Alexei agreed without a shade of remorse.

'Why did you bring me back here?' Billie pressed uneasily, utterly disconcerted by his unpredictable behaviour.

His ebony brows drew together. 'That's a silly question. You're my wife. Until I decide otherwise, this is where you belong, *yineka mou*.'

He was a Drakos and possessive of what was his. But he was talking as though she were a prized car or some other item that he owned and he would keep her close...*until I decide otherwise*. Those words of cold warning sent a cold shiver down her sensitive spine and she was no longer so certain that staying at the villa with him was the right thing to do. 'I felt more comfortable in my own home,' she told him tautly.

'Sleeping alone? Get over yourself!' Alexei

quipped with daunting disbelief, striding like a bronzed naked statue brought to life into one of the twin en suite bathrooms.

She remembered that picture of him with Calisto in Paris and discovered that she didn't want to ask him about that just at that moment. Not right now when everything felt so fragile and uncertain between them that she feared the wrong word or query might lead to a quarrel that could end their marriage for good. Her lies, her silence when she should have spoken up, had already put them on that dangerous slippery slope. Living in separate houses would not mend their differences and get them back together again, she recognised ruefully.

Even so she was walking on eggshells and could hardly bear the knowledge that to see Nicky she would have to leave the villa. It had proved a relief rather than a sacrifice to end the pretence that Hilary was Nicky's mother and, after all, she'd had only two weeks to luxuriate in the joy of being a full-time mum again for the first time since she had left London after her son's birth. And even though that fortnight had been a strain because of the situation between her and Alexei, Billie had adored having the comfort of her child within reach at all times.

Before Alexei was even out of the shower, two maids arrived with suitcases from her home. While they got busy in the dressing room, Billie went into the other bathroom with the outfit Alexei had bought for her. Thirty minutes later, she was ready for dinner and far from happy with her appearance. The scarlet dress was much more revealing than what she usually wore, cut away at the bust to make the most of what she had and very short, showing off her legs to well past mid-thigh. She checked her reflection, her brow furrowing while she wondered if the dress was a gift with a sting like a scorpion. Was this how Alexei saw her now? As a sexually provocative and available woman? As yet another in a long line of women prepared to wear whatever he bought and behave however he wanted if it pleased him?

Alexei watched Billie walk into the dining

room with keen attention. He shifted an authoritative hand to make her twirl for his appraisal and his brilliant gaze shimmered gold because he very much liked what he saw: Billie, as he had always wanted to dress her for his own private enjoyment, no longer the efficient office machine in her crisp buttoned-up blouses and low sensible pumps. Scarlet looked amazing against her porcelain redhead's skin and the cut of the dress enhanced the curves of her ripe rounded breasts and slender thighs. The reaction at his groin was instantaneous and he suppressed a groan as his trousers tightened. In that moment, he knew exactly why he had come home to reclaim his deceitful bride. Lust that powerful had an appetite and a drive all of its own.

The chef had put on a spread worthy of a banquet for the reunited couple. Nervous as a cat on hot bricks, Billie wondered how on earth she could match Alexei's stubborn refusal to acknowledge that anything was wrong between them. But, in fact, conversation flowed freely as Alexei told her about his latest deal and the changes he had decided to make in the command structure at his London headquarters. Intrigued, Billie asked eager questions, made a couple of suggestions and was duly impressed by the deal he had cut on the super-tankers.

A couple of delicious mouthfuls into the dessert she was savouring, Billie discovered that Alexei's gaze was positively welded to her. 'What?' she prompted, her face warming.

'You're a very sensual woman, *mali mou.*'

Lashes veiling her gaze, Billie shook her head in instinctive disagreement. 'I don't think so.'

Brilliant golden eyes glittering, Alexei sprang upright. 'But you just don't see yourself the way I do.' He reached down to tug her up out of her seat and bent his handsome dark head to kiss her.

Her heart was thumping so loudly she was afraid he would hear it and guess that she was a total pushover when he got that close to her. The familiar scent of him sent shivers down her spine and warmed the hollow in her tummy, leading to a shower of sharp spiky little longings in an infinitely more private place.

'I was enjoying the dessert,' she dared before his sensual mouth could connect with hers.

Eyes gleaming, Alexei threw back his a head and laughed with appreciation. 'Is this your idea of playing it cool?'

'Why would I act like that?' she traded.

'Maybe because you know how much I want you,' Alexei husked, rubbing his cheek against the extended length of her throat as he bent her head back. 'But it won't work because your heart is racing and I can feel you trembling against me, *mali mou.*'

As his lean, muscular body shifted against her, she registered the forceful swell of his erection and the heat of her desire intensified. She turned her face under his and found his mouth hungrily for herself and didn't begrudge the male satisfaction in the growling laugh that vibrated low in his throat. Suddenly all the seething emotion of the past weeks was welling up inside her with explosive effect and the glory of his mouth on hers set her alight.

Stepping back from her, Alexei closed a lean hand over hers and walked her out of the dining room. Her troubled thoughts warred against her intentions. Yet in spite of everything that had passed between them, Alexei had come home to her and he still wanted her. Wasn't that some cause for celebration? Didn't that prove that she had more of a hold on her bridegroom than she had dared to hope? But how could he simply ignore the fact that he believed she was trying to palm off some other man's child on him? She just wanted him with her...*but she wanted her son too.* She also felt guilty that she had dressed up and dined in state while Nicky was being put to bed for the night by his great-aunt.

'Shouldn't we be talking about more serious stuff?' she asked Alexei abruptly.

As if jolted by a sudden flash of lightning, Alexei swung round to rest silencing fingers against her soft mouth, preventing her from saying anything more. 'No,' he breathed harshly.

'I don't want to talk about any of it because if I have to stop and think, I would know that I shouldn't be here with you.'

That blunt admission unnerved Billie and shook her to her very core. Generally, Alexei was decisive, disciplined, tough and immovable regardless of how difficult situations became. He had never got into the emotional aspect of events. But right now she felt rather as if she were trying to deal with a split personality, a stranger. He *knew* he shouldn't be here with her? Yet here he *was*? It was as though he had built a wall between the revelations on their wedding night and the present, spelling out the fact that only his ability to blank out and suppress those revelations allowed him to be with her again now. She gazed up at him with wide green eyes full of dismay and, in a move that suggested that her vulnerable look disturbed him, Alexei lifted her up against him and crushed her berry-tinted lips beneath his with a hungry impatient fervour that put her troubled thoughts to flight.

Billie gasped as Alexei blazed a trail of kisses

across her shoulder, tugging the straps down
on her dress and burying his face in the warm
valley between the full globes of her breasts as
he urged her down on the bed. She kicked off her
shoes while his fingers slid up her thigh to the
narrow band of her thong. In a swift movement,
he wrenched the tiny garment off and tossed it
aside. Her breath caught in her throat, channelled
in urgent gasps of helpless anticipation.

Alexei was standing over her shedding his
clothes with a seething impatience that thrilled
her. Lean strong face taut, he viewed her with
scorching golden eyes. As he cast aside his shirt,
he bent down and raised her up to pull her dress
off her without unzipping it. She heard the rip
of material, for it had been a neat fit. He flicked
loose the catch on the balconette bra that had
merely acted as an extra line of suspension and,
with it gone, she was naked.

'No, don't you dare try to cover a centimetre
of that beautiful bare flesh,' Alexei censured
huskily, lifting her up the bed to settle her in a
pose that concealed nothing from his burning

gaze. 'This is what I wanted from the moment I saw you in the bath earlier. Within seconds I was hotter than hell for you, *moraki mou.*'

A high-voltage smile of extraordinary sexual power tilted his beautiful mouth and it was just as if he lit a fire inside her. In a flash Billie went from feeling hideously awkward in her unadorned skin to lying back in quivering readiness and acceptance. He wrenched off his silk boxers and came down to her. All rock-hard muscle from his magnificent torso to his flat stomach and long powerful thighs, he was hugely aroused. He brought her hand to the virile shaft rising from the thick dark curls at his groin.

Feeling the pound of the pulse at the heart of her and the moisture there, she closed her fingers round his hard male heat and watched his thick dark lashes sweep down with an uninhibited sensual pleasure that sent the blood pounding at an insane rate through her own veins. With a new boldness she drew him down to her and used her mouth to caress his straining masculinity.

Within the space of a minute he pulled back

from her. 'I can't take too much of that,' he confided, his dark deep accented drawl rough with erotic meaning. 'I want to be inside you too badly.'

And he touched her then with infinite skill, his thumb teasing her swollen bud and making her release an abandoned little cry and shiver even as a lean finger probed the slick wetness of her lush opening. As her hips bucked in a movement as old as time he entered her all too willing body with a single driving thrust. Her spine arched and her teeth clenched on the extraordinary tide of sensation as his engorged length stretched her tight inner depths.

'You feel like hot silk,' Alexei ground out, rising over her while gliding into her tender flesh with strong, stirring strokes that fuelled her growing excitement to ever greater heights.

He wanted to make it last but her sheer abandonment to pleasure and the frantic urgency of her movements pushed him to the edge very quickly and created a chain reaction. As Alexei surged into her with ever greater power, it was

too much for Billie and she soared into a convulsive orgasm, writhing and crying out with
the bittersweet pain of release. While she was
still struggling to surface from the incredible
intensity of that climax, Alexei's magnificent
body shuddered over hers in the grip of the same
overwhelming finale.

Afterwards, Billie felt emptied and adrift,
totally shattered by the intensity of what she
had just experienced. But this time, Alexei did
not pull away from her, making her feel alone
and uncertain at a most vulnerable time. Still
trembling from the explosive force of his own
release, he kept her in the circle of his strong
arms and kissed her brow in a surprisingly gentle
salutation.

'Alexei…' she whispered softly in acknowledgement, her body surrendering to her exhaus-
tion, her eyes sliding closed.

'You're worth going to hell and back for,' he
murmured with growling carnal satisfaction.
'Nobody has ever given me that much excitement, *moraki mou*.'

And Billie drifted off to sleep in his arms, happier than she had ever dreamed she might be after that awful nerve-racking two weeks apart from him. The sex was amazing, she was willing to agree, but that tender kiss and his relaxation with her in the aftermath meant a great deal more to her. She wondered if she would ever fully understand the man she loved. He was so complex, volatile and in every respect unpredictable. And on that frustrated acknowledgement she sank into the deepest sleep she had enjoyed in many weeks.

She awakened, befogged by drowsiness and bewildered, to the bright light of an island morning. Alexei, fully dressed, was standing over the bed.

'Is there no end to your deceptions?' he demanded of her in savage condemnation.

Astonished by that attack, Billie pushed herself up clumsily against the pillows, suddenly conscious of her nudity and holding the sheet to her breasts. Running trembling fingers through her wildly tousled red hair to rake it back off her face, she mumbled, 'What are you talking about? What's wrong?'

'*This*…this is what's wrong!' Alexei bit out rawly, flinging a newspaper down on the bed for her to look at. 'You and Damon Marios holding hands on my private beach!'

Her face stiff with shock, Billie glanced down at the page and froze, her skin turning clammy, her throat closing over. It was not the best photo she had ever seen and it seemed to have been digitally enhanced for clarity, but it did show her and Damon on the beach, clearly engaged in intent conversation, her hand in his, her face turned up to his. She was dismayed to recognise that even though her dialogue with Damon had been entirely innocent of even flirtation the photo was misleading, as was the closeness of their bodies.

She flung her head back, green eyes very bright. 'This is not what it looks like,' she whispered shakily.

CHAPTER FIVE

'IT WAS taken by a telephoto lens. The paparazzo must've been in a boat,' Alexei grated between clenched teeth, and then he swept the newspaper off the bed again in an angry gesture of repudiation. 'What the hell is going on between you and Marios? Is he the father of your baby?'

'No, he is not. We're friends, nothing more. All that happened between us was a rather emotional conversation. Damon was telling me why his marriage had ended.'

'Exchanging sob stories, were you? Getting all touchy-feely?' Alexei glowered at her unimpressed, his lean dark features hard with angry denunciation. 'I don't believe you. Damon was your first love and you've always had a thing for him. I can well understand too why you would want to conceal your child's identity on

Speros after Damon chose to reconcile with his estranged wife last year.'

At that crack, Billie turned very pale, for it struck her as terrifying that it could take only one piece of misinformation to provide a foundation for a seemingly convincing case against her. 'I've never been intimate with Damon. He is *not* the father of my child,' she intoned afresh, desperate to make Alexei listen to her.

Alexei swore only half under his breath. '*Na pas sto dialo!* Go to hell,' he told her roughly. 'I'm leaving. In a couple of days the DNA results will be available and I refuse to see you again until then.'

In consternation, Billie watched him stride towards the door. 'Where are you going?'

'London. I'll see you at Hazlehurst in forty-eight hours,' he spelt out grimly.

He didn't even have to pack, Billie acknowledged limply, because Alexei kept capsule wardrobes all over the world at the properties he used the most. He was walking out on her again. After a night that had filled her with a crazy burst of hope for the future, he was leaving and she was devastated by that development.

It was the work of an instant to run to the door and shout furiously down the corridor after him, 'You're a total coward, Alexei Drakos!'

She knew that hurling that accusation at a proud Greek male was like waving a red flag in front of a maddened bull and, sure enough, her tall, muscular husband wheeled straight round in his tracks to throw her an outraged look of incredulity from fierce golden eyes.

'I mean it…every word!' she flung in provocative addition, only belatedly becoming conscious that she was stark naked, and closing the door hurriedly to seek something to wear.

And true to the arrogant Drakos tradition of fearless confrontation, Alexei powered back down the corridor again and thrust the bedroom door back open so violently that it crashed back against the wall. Halfway into his discarded shirt, Billie faltered. She had never seen him so irate, his eyes blazing above the patrician cheekbones showing prominent and pale beneath his bronzed skin, his lean hands clenched into fists. 'How dare you accuse me of such behaviour?'

'Because you've been running away ever since I told you the truth about our child. You left the yacht on our wedding night and you're leaving me now, walking out all over again,' she condemned bitterly. 'How does that solve anything? Last night you wouldn't even talk. You won't discuss anything with me!'

'What the hell is there to discuss?' Alexei raked back at her in a lion's roar of intimidation that made her tremble, his powerful stance as aggressive as it was dogmatic. 'You've told me nothing but stupid stories that a child could tear apart.'

'Those were not stupid stories!'

Alexei came several steps closer. 'You've lied and lied and lied again to me,' he derided. 'Why do you think I would want to listen to more of the same?'

'I *had* to lie…I didn't know what else to do,' she shot back at him shrilly. 'Why does everything have to be about you? What do you think

it was like for me when you took up with Calisto
and told me you were thinking about marrying
her?'

Alexei stretched out his arms and then dropped
them again in a volatile gesture of frustration and
impatience. 'I'm not listening to this nonsense
again. Nothing you have told me justifies your
behaviour. You've got nothing left to say. Lies are
lies, no matter what the circumstances. I won't
live with them or forgive them.'

White with anger, he studied her standing there
in his half-buttoned shirt, her tangle of colourful
red hair spread round her shoulders. He dealt her
a bitter look of cynicism. 'We're over, we've got
to be. Sizzling sex isn't enough to keep me with
you,' he delivered with harsh emphasis, and this
time when he turned to leave she said nothing
and she made no attempt to bring him back.

That evening after Billie had tucked Nicky up
for the night in her own home, she found herself
engaged in a bitter debate with her mother.

'Your marriage is already over bar the shouting,' Lauren told her daughter sourly.

'Of course it isn't,' Billie reasoned. 'Once Alexei realises that Nicky is his son...'

'He's not like his father who was desperate for an heir,' the older woman pointed out bluntly. 'You're so naïve, Billie. Men aren't driven to be fathers the same way women are driven to be mothers. It's different for them, so wise up. Alexei has already told you that the marriage is over and in my opinion the discovery that he has a kid isn't going to change that.'

'You're such a pessimist,' Hilary scolded her sister from the lamp-lit corner where she had been trying to read a book.

'Billie has to look out for her own interests now,' Lauren argued forcefully. 'Alexei consulted his lawyers when he organised that DNA test. Billie should see a good divorce lawyer while she's in the UK. Hilary, stop looking at me like I just took an axe to Santa Claus! Alexei is a Drakos—let's face it, her marriage was always going to end in tears. His father only finally settled down because he was getting too old to stray and you can't hope for that with a guy who's only thirty-one.'

Billie breathed in deep. In truth she was finding her mother's ominous predictions more than she could comfortably cope with just at that moment. She offered to make some supper and went out to the kitchen, for she had already learned that the only way to keep a grip on her worries was to physically *do* something. Idleness while she had nothing but anxious thoughts whirling inside her head had become a torment. Much as she loved Nicky, she missed the buzz of working.

She was taking Nicky to Hazlehurst with her and had already arranged for Anatalya's daughter, Kasma, to travel with her and help her look after her son. After all, unlike Alexei, Billie already knew the results of the DNA test and she was convinced that she and Alexei would have a lot to talk about. She was praying that Alexei would find himself more interested in being a parent than her sceptical mother had forecast. A child could bring them together again, couldn't

it? Unfortunately she remembered reading somewhere that a child only made matters worse in a
failing relationship and she could only hope that
Nicky would have a more positive effect on their
marriage. Surely Alexei would not divorce her
for being the mother of his only child?

The following day while she was engaged
in packing for their trip to England, Anatalya
brought her a letter, addressed to her as Alexei's
wife but heavily marked private and confidential.
Opening the missive, she sank down on the bed
to read it after her eyes flew wide on the first
shocking sentence, 'I believe it is possible that I
may be your father...'

Slowly and carefully, Billie read the letter. For
all its startling opening, it was a remarkably sensible and far from dramatic communication in
which its writer, Desmond Bury, explained that
he had fallen in love with her mother, Lauren,
when she'd come to work as a teenage recep-
tionist at his father's vehicle-repair garage. An
engagement had followed during which Lauren
had fallen pregnant. Sadly, by then, Lauren had

decided that she no longer wanted to marry Desmond and, having told him that she intended to seek a termination, she had dumped him for another man. He'd had no further contact with Lauren until he'd come upon a newspaper article about Billie's engagement to Alexei, which had also featured a picture of her with Lauren. Ever since he had been wondering if Billie could be his daughter, for her age and colouring fitted that scenario. The letter concluded with a small paragraph on Desmond's history. He had eventually married and was now the widowed owner of a flourishing chain of garages. If Billie believed that she might be his daughter, he would like the opportunity to meet and get to know her.

Five minutes after her third reading of the missive, Billie drove down to the village with Nicky to see her mother and handed her the letter. 'Is there any truth in this? Is it possible that this man could be my father? Were you once engaged to him?'

Lauren grimaced and rolled her eyes theatrically several times while she read the letter. 'Yes to all those questions,' she said grudgingly. 'But he's got no right telling you that I considered a termination while I was carrying you…'

'I think he may only have mentioned that because he wanted me to know that he would have taken an interest in me sooner had he known I existed,' Billie responded mildly. 'And I don't blame you for considering it…'

'Well, you can thank Hilary for the fact I didn't go ahead with it!' Lauren fielded tight-mouthed. 'But I've got no regrets where Desmond was concerned. He was a bore, middle aged at twenty-five, a pipe-and-slippers man, not my type at all.'

'So why, when I was a teenager, did you tell me that I was the result of a one-night stand?' Billie asked painfully. 'That upset me and I honestly thought you didn't know *who* my father was.'

Lauren laughed heartily at that candid admission. 'I thought you would blame me for not marrying Desmond and giving you a more conventional childhood.'

'I'm glad you didn't marry him just for the

sake of it,' Billie told the older woman truthfully. 'It would never have worked out if you were so different.'

'Will you get in touch with Desmond?' Lauren prompted with a frown. 'You know, he's really not an exciting person.'

'If he is my father, I would like to meet him.'

'Oh, he is definitely your father,' Lauren confirmed with a sigh, as if she was more embarrassed than anything else by that.

The next day Billie arrived in London and climbed into the limo that would waft her, Nicky and Kasma to Hazlehurst. She had dressed with care in a beautifully elegant dark purple suit, rescued from looking like office apparel by a short skirt, high heels and snappy accessories. Kasma, who had only been abroad once before, was excited by everything she saw while Nicky looked adorable in a practical blue-striped playsuit and little jacket. The closer they came to their final destination, the more nervous Billie became.

Basking in early summer sunlight, Hazlehurst looked idyllic. The house wore its Georgian

beginnings with style and elegance. The redoubt-
able housekeeper looked surprised when Billie
arrived with a child in tow but wasted no time in
calling another member of staff to escort Kasma
and her charge upstairs to the nursery floor. Even
before Billie was directed into the drawing room
to see Alexei, her tummy was rolling and her
skin dampening with nervous perspiration.

The tall front windows had a wonderful view
of the lawns that ran below beech trees clad in
the fresh green of their seasonal finery. Poised to
one side of that view, Alexei looked formidable,
sheathed in a dark pinstripe business suit of flaw-
less cut and tailoring. His lean, darkly handsome
face was taut and unrevealing, but his brilliant
eyes glittered with a light that warned her that
appearances could be deceptive, and that he was
by no means as calm as he might seem on the
surface. Alexei was, after all, studying her as if
he had never quite seen her before.

'You...*know*,' Billie guessed immediately, her
voice emerging strangely squeaky and insub-
stantial from her lips. Even when he intimidated

her, he could still take her breath away with his stark male beauty and high-voltage sexual magnetism. No matter what thoughts ran through her anxious mind, at the back of those thoughts she was recalling the hard driving rhythm of his lean powerful body on and inside hers and the ecstasy of release that had allowed her, for such a brief time, to feel close to him. Was it any wonder that her throat was dry and her lungs reluctant to give her more oxygen?

'I received the DNA results early this morning. At first I couldn't credit it,' Alexei imparted between compressed lips, more than a hint of ferocious self-discipline still etched in his tense stance and forbidding aspect.

'You should have known I wouldn't lie about something that was so easily proven one way or other,' Billie dared, lifting her chin in challenge. 'Of course, Nicky is your child.'

'But I remember nothing,' Alexei growled in a driven undertone, his incapacity in that field evidently now a source of deep resentment. 'Although I now know it obviously happened, it's still a challenge for me to accept that I slept with you that night and that I was so careless that I got you pregnant.'

Dismayed by that punishing choice of wording, Billie flinched. 'All I can say is that we were both upset and vulnerable that evening and when we were together it didn't feel wrong or out of place.'

His intense stare made her feel as though he would like to get inside her memory of that evening and take it from her rather than simply share it with her. She sensed his duality in the strong current of aggression that still ran beneath his self-disciplined surface and wondered at it. He was not reacting to the revelation of Nicky's paternity as she had hoped or expected and yet she could not have said precisely what was wrong with his attitude.

'I don't want platitudes from you. I want to know exactly what happened between us…'

Unsure as to what he meant by that statement, Billie worried at her lower lip with her teeth. 'The *obvious* happened—'

She collided with unrelenting dark golden eyes. 'I want to know what I did, what I said, what you did—every detail,' Alexei told her flatly.

Embarrassment swallowed Billie whole and glued her tongue to the roof of her mouth. 'I don't remember much,' she fibbed in desperation.

Alexei dealt her a gleaming look of contempt. 'Just another forgettable shag, was I?'

'I wouldn't know about that—I don't have anyone to compare you to!' Billie snapped back at him furiously. 'I was a virgin.'

Alexei nodded acceptance of that fact. 'Okay, so talk…'

Billie wandered restively over to the window and turned her narrow back to him in self-defence. In truth she had near-perfect recall of their time together and she repeated snatches of conversation and mentioned the sharing of the shower and the reason for his departure. 'I think you fell down the steps because you tripped over my handbag…I'd dropped it on the floor by the door on the way in,' she completed woodenly.

The silence stretched and gnawed at her nerves.

Throwing back her head, vivid coppery hair falling back from her pale cheeks and brow, Billie straightened her stiff shoulders and spun back to him. 'So, now you know that Nicky is your son—'

Her husband's lean powerful visage hardened from the reflective look he had worn. 'And I so easily might never have known,' he interrupted. 'Had I married Calisto, you would *never* have told me—'

She was alert to the renewed tension in the atmosphere. Billie's spine went rigid and a smidgeon of colour warmed her cheeks. 'I don't know what I would have done if you had married her,' she contradicted.

An ebony brow quirked, for he was unimpressed by that claim. 'Don't you? You would have deprived me of my son, denied my son his father and disinherited him of his Drakos heritage,' he condemned, taking her breath away with those hard-hitting charges. 'Both he and I would have paid a very steep price for our ignorance of our bond. Were you planning to lie to him when he got old enough to ask who his father was?'

'I hadn't got that far, for goodness' sake. I hadn't even thought about stuff like that!' Billie disclaimed in a tone of unconscious appeal. 'Nicky's only a baby—'

Alexei raised his head high, dark golden eyes hard with censure. 'Nikolos is my son and you passed him off as someone else's, even brought him into my home in that false guise. As a mother, you failed in your duty to him.'

Shaken by those accusations, Billie felt her cheeks grow hot. 'And as a wife?' she chipped in helplessly.

'You leave more than a little to be desired,' Alexei delivered without hesitation and he swung open the drawing-room door and stood back with contrasting courtesy for her exit. 'Now I would like to see my son. At least you had the good sense to bring him here with you.'

Billie felt rather as if a whip had somehow contrived to lash her skin below her clothes. Anger sparking, she tried to defend herself. 'In my position some women would have opted for a termination and your son would never have been born.'

'Maybe you saw his existence as money in the bank for a future power-play. Certainly that is how your mother thinks and don't try to tell me otherwise. Lauren is always out for what she can get.'

At that cruel taunt, her delicate facial bones tightened below her fair skin and her fingernails bit sharp crescents of restraint into her palms, because she truly wanted to shout and scream at him for daring to make that humiliating comparison. He had never in his life before compared her to her feckless and avaricious parent, and that he should do so now hurt like the sharp slice of a knife in already tender flesh. 'I'm not like my mother and you know I'm not.'

Crossing the big echoing hall on his passage to the grand staircase, Alexei skimmed a cool glance at her taut profile. 'Once I would have agreed with that statement, but not any more. I don't know you the way I thought I knew you.'

A lump formed in her throat. 'I don't feel I know you either just at this moment.'

'I'm still very angry with you,' Alexei responded with succinct bite. 'Of course I am. I've already missed out on months of my child's life and I'm a complete stranger to him.'

Mounting the stairs by his side, Billie murmured, 'I thought you weren't ready for a child.'

'He's *here*, ready or not!' Alexei quipped with derision.

'I didn't realise you'd feel this way.'

'Until I found out about Nikolos, neither did I,' Alexei admitted in a raw undertone. 'But he's the next generation of my family and his beginnings couldn't have been worse! He's my responsibility and the buck stops here.'

Ouch, Billie thought at that far-reaching assumption of responsibility but she said nothing, recognising that he had to have a lot of conflicting feelings to work through and that in many ways he was probably still in shock at the result of the DNA test. All of a sudden he had been plunged into fatherhood and the smokescreen with which she had surrounded Nicky's birth and paternity only complicated that state of affairs.

Kasma was playing with Nicky on the floor of the well-appointed nursery. Alexei told the nursemaid to take a break and the young Greek woman had barely crossed the threshold when he bent down to scoop his son up off the carpet. Taken by surprise, Nicky loosed a startled yell of complaint and scowled at his father.

'He can be a bit strange at present; he's not comfortable with anyone he doesn't know,' Billie warned him reluctantly, mentally willing Nicky to be compliant and friendly at this crucial first meeting with his father.

Alexei drew his son awkwardly closer and Nicky burst into noisy floods of tears and wrenched his little body dramatically sideways in his mother's direction.

Billie reached out to take her distraught son into her arms. 'Try playing with him first,' she suggested.

'I've never played with a kid in my life,'

Alexei said flatly. 'Is he always this jumpy or is it just me?'

'Babies can be very sensitive to atmosphere and we're both fairly tense.'

Alexei studied his son's truculent little face with intense interest. He scanned the baby's tousled black hair, his olive skin tone, his big dark accusing eyes and the manner in which he was clinging to his mother. Alexei wondered how he hadn't guessed that Nikolos was his child for, in his opinion, the physical resemblance was marked. How come some sixth-sense prompting hadn't urged him to take a closer look at Billie's supposed cousin? How come he hadn't tied together the evidence of her unexplained sickness as reported by Anatalya and her months-long career break, which had come out of nowhere at him? But he knew exactly why he hadn't put it all together.

He had had no recollection of their sexual encounter and he had trusted her absolutely while she had gone to extraordinary lengths to deceive him: there was no getting round that unpleasant truth.

Billie lifted up a picture book and pushed it into Alexei's hand. 'That's Nicky's favourite. I'll put him in the baby seat and you can read it and show him the pictures.'

'Surely he's still too young for stories?'

'He always looks interested and stays quiet while I read to him. Babies like familiar rituals.'

With a strong air of reluctance, his lean dark features tense, Alexei sank down in the armchair beside the baby seat and leant down to Nicky's level. 'You don't have to stay,' Alexei told Billie. 'I don't need an audience for this.'

Billie would have preferred to stay to act as a buffer and a source of advice, but then Alexei had always been very self-sufficient in the face of a challenge. She walked out of the door and closed it, listened outside as her son started to sob at her departure and heaved a sigh as she moved away again. If there was a lesson to be learned, Alexei would only learn it the hard way and at his own pace.

Alexei had never had to entertain a child before, but his quick intelligence soon came to his aid. In no time he had the box full of toys by the wall emptied and he was demonstrating the different items for his son's amusement. The tears dried on the little boy's face as he slowly responded to that stimulation. He smiled when Alexei got him out of the baby seat and sat him on the carpet instead. He gurgled with pleasure when Alexei showed him the different noises one toy made and stretched out his hand for it, pummelling it with a chubby fist, only to start complaining when he couldn't get the same sound to emerge. Alexei showed him again and took a little fist and showed him where to press. Nikolos chortled with satisfaction, thumped the toy energetically several times with his clenched hand and then suddenly held out his arms to Alexei to be lifted.

Kneeling on the carpet in front of his son, absently wondering when he would be old enough to appreciate mechanical toys, Alexei froze at that unexpected invitation. The baby gave him a huge grin and, ending his hesitation, Alexei moved forward and lifted him. Nikolos grabbed his father's tie and yanked it, and then put it in his mouth to chew. Alexei deprived him of the tie, sprang up to find a source of distraction and found it in the view from the window. While he was showing his son the trees, the tractor and the sheep that were visible, the little boy laughed and tried to copy him and point his own fingers, brown eyes full of life and fun.

And, for Alexei, that unstudied moment of shared relaxation suddenly became one of the most important and emotionally gripping of his life. Only a few hours earlier he had decided that he was still too young and selfish to be a parent. At the speed of light he had worked out all the drawbacks of parenthood, swiftly recognising the boundaries that would now be imposed on his once free and untrammelled lifestyle. He might have had no experience of young children but he certainly knew enough to know that a child was major baggage.

But now memories were surfacing of his own father and with them a rich appreciation of the fact that *he* was still young enough to fully understand what his child would enjoy and to actually play with him. Constantine Drakos had never, ever played with his son and had treated him like a miniature adult. Their relationship had always been sedate and a little detached with Alexei's mother cheerfully supplying the glue of family affection and all the fun.

Ten minutes later Alexei was sitting with Nikolos on his lap and he was reading the few words in the picture book and, what was more, he was bringing an excitement to that familiar pastime, for Alexei mimicked the noises the different animals made when Billie had merely read them.

When Billie reappeared an hour after her departure, all was quiet in the nursery. Alexei moved a silencing finger to his mouth; their son was fast asleep in his arms, as relaxed as if he had known his father from the day of his birth. Both surprised and pleased by that discovery, Billie smiled warmly, relief uppermost. She had no idea what Alexei had done to win the little boy's trust but, whatever it was, he had clearly done it well.

'I am grateful you had him,' Alexei admitted outside the door and as she gazed up at him, a vulnerable light in her emerald-green eyes, his handsome mouth compressed. 'But he deserved that you should have told me the truth right at the beginning of your pregnancy.'

Her eyes veiled. 'Maybe so.'

His lean, strong face clenched hard. 'You know better than that. I have work to catch up on before dinner,' he responded, heading for the stairs, making no attempt to hide his exasperation with her.

Grovelling didn't come naturally to her, Billie recognised ruefully as she entered the master bedroom to decide what to wear for their evening meal. He remained angry with her, while refusing to accept that she had grounds for being angry with him as well. There were two sides to every story. He needed to acknowledge that his partial amnesia had put her in an untenable and humiliating position and then Calisto's arrival on the scene had proved to be the last straw. She had given birth to their child without his support and the deep unhappiness and loneliness that she had endured during the long months of her pregnancy still haunted her. Hilary had been marvellous but her company had also made Billie feel that she had to act as if she were a good deal happier and more positive than she actually was. For months she had lived behind a false face and had maintained that she was feeling fine.

Desperate to escape the circuitous anxiety of her thoughts, Billie took out her father's letter and read it again. She decided to phone Desmond Bury there and then, have a chat and see how she felt about him without making a major production out of establishing contact. After all, Desmond might be her father but he was also a stranger with whom she might have nothing whatsoever in common. At the same time, however, she and her mother were so different that she could not help hoping that she might find something of her own nature reflected in her other parent.

Her heart was in her mouth when she made the call and a crisp businesslike male voice answered on the fourth ring. She heard his surprise when he realised who she was and then, with an endearing warmth and enthusiasm that touched her, he aimed a flurry of eager questions at her. He was surprised when she told him that she had a son and marvelled that there had been no mention of Nicky's existence in the newspaper article he had read. When she admitted that she was actually in England, rather than Greece, he asked if she would like to meet him and in receipt of a positive response immediately offered to get together with her in London. She arranged to meet him the very next day for lunch.

Proud that she had had the courage to make that phone call, Billie showered and set out black silk trousers and a sapphire-blue evening top to wear, before lifting a magazine she had bought at the airport to read. She frowned with distaste when she came on a little newsy segment on Calisto, photographed looking every inch a top model dressed in the latest fashion and talking about how much she loved living in Paris. Billie stilled and studied the building in the backdrop of the photo, which struck her as familiar. It dawned on her that she knew that street, knew it really well because she had on several occasions visited the splendid town house that Alexei owned there. Just as suddenly she was recalling that photo of Alexei with Calisto in Paris and appreciating that the pavement café they had been patronising could well be the one she recalled being just round the corner from the town house.

Could Calisto currently be living in Alexei's Parisian home?

Or were the photos just a ghastly coincidence? His town house was, after all, situated in a very trendy and photogenic part of Paris. Was insecurity making her suffer from increasingly paranoid suspicions? Billie grimaced. Suspicions about the fidelity of a male whom every paparazzo in Europe nourished suspicions about? A guy to whom fidelity was a dirty word, if it came between him and a woman he wanted? *Of course*, she was suspicious. Alexei might have married her, but he hadn't come with any cast-iron guarantee of loyalty and there was every possibility that he saw her lies and deceit over Nicky as an excuse to stray. Hadn't he already told her that they as a couple were *over*?

Just how had she contrived to overlook that fact? *We're over, we've got to be*, he had said before flying to London. Her mother, Lauren, who rarely suffered from rose-tinted glasses when it came to the male sex, had believed her daughter's marriage was already over as well. Only Billie had been naïve enough to arrive at Hazlehurst, groomed within an inch of her life, in the foolish hope that Alexei, having discovered that Nicky was his son, might greet her with apologies, understanding and forgiveness.

CHAPTER SIX

LATER, before dinner that evening, Alexei called Billie on the house phone, told her that two of the business team were off sick and asked her if she would mind helping out for a while.

Billie was quick to agree and stayed only long enough in the bedroom to dress in casual clothes. In the ground-floor office suite, she stepped into the working role she had given up as if she had never been away and although the other staff were now somewhat overawed by her new position as Alexei's wife she very much enjoyed being kept busy.

'I miss working,' she told Alexei when she joined him later for dinner, having finally donned her slinky evening trousers and blue top.

Supremely handsome in his dark suit, Alexei surveyed her slight figure and the bright hair flaming round her pale heart-shaped face and his wide sensual mouth compressed. 'But you're a mother now.'

'Surely I could still work part-time with you?' Billie prompted, longing for the closeness of that working relationship to be restored.

'Not when I'm travelling,' Alexei pointed out drily.

And Billie *had* overlooked that necessity when she'd come up with her proposition. While she was ready to allow her son to be cared for several hours a day, she was not prepared to leave him for several days at a time or to disrupt his routine by taking him travelling round the world with her.

'But your talent for efficient organisation and working well under pressure is much missed,' Alexei conceded wryly.

'I think I could still work several hours a day from the villa without Nicky suffering any deprivation,' Billie responded with quiet determination.

His brilliant dark eyes lingered on the obstinate

set of her small face and his lush lashes screened his gaze. 'I'll think it over.'

'When you talk to me like that—as if I haven't a brain or self-will of my own and I'm a possession—I want to slap you hard!' Billie confided in a rush, pushing her chair noisily back from the table and leaping upright in a temper.

Refusing to rise to the bait, Alexei surveyed her steadily with his stunning dark golden eyes. 'With reference to most of the decisions you have made over the past year and more, I cannot be impressed.'

Billie gritted her teeth and shot him a look of frustration. 'Did you think Calisto was more impressive?' she dared in a driven voice.

His strong jaw line clenched. 'I have no intention of discussing Calisto with you.'

Her angry flush receding at that wounding snub, Billie muttered, 'I'm tired. I'm going to bed.'

Coward, she scolded herself once she was lying in the lavish marital bed. Why hadn't she mentioned that photo of him with Calisto in

Paris? Asked where Calisto was staying over there? Yet without proof of anything untoward, what would be the point of questioning Alexei? He would very much resent an interrogation. And with their marriage hanging in the balance did she really want to take the risk of heightening the conflict between them? Of making counter-accusations that might well have no basis in reality? Alexei had still to apologise for suspecting her of a secret affair with Damon Marios, she reminded herself doggedly. She tossed and turned while she swung between angry defiance, fear of losing Alexei and self-loathing. She loved him too much, still wanted him too much in spite of the way he was treating her, and that made her despise herself. Oh, how she longed to reclaim the sensible wall of detachment she had once been able to protect herself with around Alexei!

Alexei was considerate enough not to put on the lights when he came to bed after midnight, but when he swore after colliding with a solid piece of furniture in the darkness Billie stretched up with a sigh to switch on the bedside lights. 'It's all right…I'm not asleep,' she told him.

She tried to go to sleep then, but when the mattress sank beneath his weight, she said abruptly, 'Did you really think I'd got involved with Damon?' That demand came to her lips before she even appreciated that she needed to ask him it.

'I was with Calisto. How do I know what you did during that period? Or whether you would turn to him for sympathy when our marriage was in trouble?' he fielded stonily.

'Well, you could start by trying not to assume that everything I say is a lie,' Billie pointed out gently. 'Just because I found Damon attractive when I was a teenager doesn't mean I still feel the same way as an adult—'

'Why not? He so obviously *does* still find you tempting,' Alexei retorted drily.

That response filled her with impatience over his obstinacy. She was damned if she did, damned if she didn't. 'There's just one flaw in that view. I'm in love with you,' she said boldly.

'If hiding my child from me is your idea of love, I can live without it. Trust is more important and we've lost it,' he delivered bluntly, turning out the lights again.

As his lean powerful body brushed up against hers Billie froze like an icicle; his take on their marriage chilled her to the marrow. He didn't love her, he didn't even want her love and he didn't trust her either. Did that leave anything left for her to hope for? Any bond with which they might rebuild their relationship? Alexei closed an arm round her and tugged her up close in a movement that took her totally by surprise and reminded her of a potential fringe benefit of matrimony that she had overlooked. The sensitive tips of her breasts swelled and tightened in contact with his hard muscular torso and a sensation like hot liquid lightning snaked through her pelvis, creating moisture on the tender flesh between her slender thighs. His mouth brushed her cheek, his breath fanning her lips, and the musky male scent of him flared her nostrils and left her weaker still. But her defences conjured up that photo of him seated with Calisto in Paris and somewhere down deep inside herself she was able to switch off the current of responsive heat and turn colder than a winter's day in his arms.

'No,' she breathed in fierce rejection.

Alexei tensed. *'No?'*

And a part of her that she didn't like very much gloried in his lack of familiarity with that negative word between the sheets. She pushed him away and retreated to the far edge of the bed. 'No. Feeling as you do about me, I don't think you should be touching me,' she extended in blunt clarification.

Without warning the lights went on again and she blinked in astonishment. Alexei sent her a seething appraisal, his lean dark features hard as iron. 'You're not going to punish me with celibacy, *glikia mou*!'

'That's not what I'm trying to do!' she snapped back, even while she wondered if it actually was and if sometimes he saw her more clearly than she saw herself.

Alexei flung back the sheet and strode naked and still heavily aroused into the bathroom. Seconds later she heard the shower running and she lay there very still for quite a while until he finally reappeared, a towel negligently knotted round his narrow hips. Green eyes wide with consternation, she studied him over the top of the sheet. She could feel his anger like a physical force in the atmosphere and was already wondering if she had made a mistake in refusing him what she wanted herself. But she was ashamed of the fact that regardless of what he said and how he behaved he only had to get close for her to crave him with every fibre of her being.

'We can't make love with everything so wrong between us,' she muttered in urgent appeal.

A sardonic expression stamped to his darkly handsome features, Alexei shot her a harsh narrowed glance of condemnation. 'Who said anything about making love?' he repeated the expression with silken derision. 'I was talking about sex. You think separate beds are likely to help us?'

'Sex isn't the answer to everything!' Billie slung back in frustration.

Alexei looked grim as he walked to the door. 'No, but it's important to me, to *any* man!'

'Where on earth are you going?' Billie gasped.

'I don't want to run the risk of waking up tomorrow morning and treating you as if you're my wife,' he derided. 'So I'll sleep elsewhere.'

Tears stung her eyes at the prospect of that cold physical separation. She wasn't at all sure about what she had just done but his refusal to even countenance the term 'making love' for their intimacy had hit hard and had bolstered up her defences. At the same time she just couldn't get Calisto out of her mind and his refusal to talk about his ex-fiancée only increased her doubts about the nature of his continuing relationship with the other woman. In one way Alexei had been very right: the trust they had once shared had gone and without it she felt lost, scared and out of control.

When she awakened early the next morning,

Alexei had already left the house. She had to phone Helios to discover that her husband had flown out to France, a revelation that shook her inside out. As soon as she heard it she was convinced that he would be staying in Paris with Calisto and spending the night with the gorgeous blonde. That conviction killed her appetite for breakfast and made it a major challenge for her to feed Nicky and play with him with her usual light heart. Worry stoked her growing anger. Possibly freezing Alexei out of the marital bedroom the night before had been unwise, but he had blocked all her efforts to bridge the mental gulf between them. If he imagined, however, that she planned to close her eyes to his infidelity as so many other women had in the past he was in for a huge shock! Determined to discover the truth at first hand, Billie booked a late afternoon flight to Paris. If Alexei had resumed his affair with Calisto, she would confront them and see the evidence for herself before she gave up hope on their marriage.

After all that drama and agonising over what

to do next it was an effort for Billie to get into the right frame of mind to go and meet her long-lost father for the first time. When she realised that a security team was to accompany her to London, she swiftly appreciated that if she accepted their presence she would never be able to surprise Alexei with Calisto in Paris as he would immediately be informed if she was flying into the same city. So, when Petros joined her in the hall to request exact details of her planned itinerary in London, she told him that she was sorry but that she did not wish to be accompanied.

'I'm following your husband's orders, *kyria*,' Petros replied in some surprise. 'It is the wish of Kyrios Drakos that you enjoy protection whenever you leave home.'

'But I'm afraid it is not my wish,' Billie replied firmly. 'You may tell my husband that I refused to allow you to come with me.'

Feeling guilty at having put the bewildered Petros in that awkward position, Billie left Hazlehurst without any further ado. Just before Billie got out of the limo at the rural station where she was to catch a train to the city, Alexei called her on her mobile phone.

'What the hell are you playing at?' he demanded without any preliminary chat. 'You *need* a security team—'

'I don't need anyone following me every place I go. I like my privacy.'

'Privacy in which to do what?' Alexei queried in a glancing challenge that startled her.

Billie released an angry laugh. 'So now we're getting to the truth of the matter. It's not my personal safety you're concerned about, but what I might be doing. You want me to have bodyguards so that you can spy on me and I won't accept that!'

Buoyed up with a sense that she had to stand up for her rights before Alexei's powerful personality and controlling nature steamrollered her bid for independence flat as a pancake, Billie switched off her mobile phone and plunged it back into her bag. She caught the train to London and walked to meet her father in a quiet restaurant that lay not far from the station.

Her first impressions of Desmond Bury were good and her tension slowly began to drain away. She found unexpected pleasure in the fact that she had evidently inherited her father's small stature, auburn hair and green eyes. Smartly dressed in what was obviously a new suit, the older man felt familiar from the first moment he joined her with a rather shy smile at her table. He asked her a great deal about her childhood experiences on Speros and she wrapped up the truth as best she could, while suspecting that he had known Lauren well enough to deduce that her daughter might well be glossing over some disagreeable realities. In turn Desmond answered Billie's questions about his side of the family tree and his business. His marriage had been child-less and his parents were long dead so, with the exception of a couple of elderly great-aunts in Scotland, there were no other close relatives for her to discover. Billie asked him if he thought they should get a DNA test to confirm their rela-tionship and he looked taken aback momentarily. Then he grasped her hand firmly to assure her that she was the very picture of his late sister and that he was already fully satisfied that she was his flesh and blood. His unquestioning faith in their bond warmed her heart as much as Alexei's distrust had chilled it.

Lunch lasted much longer than Billie had originally planned and she parted from her father only after accepting an invitation for her and Nicky to spend a weekend at his home in Brighton. She was grateful that he had not asked awkward questions about her marriage and only realised afterwards that having confided that Alexei knew nothing about their get-together had probably revealed more than she would have preferred to have admitted about the state of her marriage.

In early summer, Paris was packed with tourists and the traffic from the airport was heavy. Desperate to escape the stuffy cab and calm her frantic thoughts, Billie chose to be dropped a block from Alexei's elegant eighteenth century town house on Ile St-Louis. The tree-lined quai could not have looked more attractive in the sunlight but Billie had never been less aware of the beauty of the ancient buildings because she was a bag of nerves beset by doubts and insecurities.

As she approached the steps to the imposing front door, she asked herself what she was most afraid of. Was it of what she would find, or of having to deal with the fallout from a husband's extra-marital affair? That latter discovery would mean the death of hope and the end of their marriage, but she could not live in fear; she had to know one way or another if Alexei had resumed his affair with Calisto. She rang the doorbell before she could think better of it.

Calisto answered the door. Luxuriant blonde hair waving round her slim shoulders, her big dark eyes haughtily enquiring, her tall slender body was sheathed in a stretchy miniskirt and top ensemble that was provocatively tight and short. Her gaze hardened as she recognised her caller. 'What are you doing here?' she demanded baldly.

'As this is Alexei's house, I think I could

more easily ask you that,' Billie dared to reply in Greek, trying not to be intimidated by the reality that the beautiful blonde towered over her like an adult beside a small child. 'I would like to come in.'

Calisto dealt her a scornful glance and, turning on her heel, walked away from the door, leaving it open. 'If you feel you must…'

'I do,' Billie replied, closing the door behind her with a trembling hand. 'Alexei isn't here, is he?'

Calisto cast her a maddeningly amused smile. 'He will be soon. Feel free to sit down and wait. I would enjoy being a fly on the wall at that meeting.'

Icily calm on the surface, Billie lifted her chin. 'I'm not afraid of you.'

Calisto released a scornful and unimpressed laugh. 'Of course you are—why else would you be here?'

As the other woman's laugh echoed eerily in the cool marble hallway with its high ceiling nausea stirred in Billie's stomach. She felt lost and hopeless and the very thought of being found in the town house with Calisto by Alexei made her blood run cold. All of a sudden she had no very clear idea why she had decided that she had to confront Calisto face to face, or of what she had come to Paris to say. *Leave Alexei alone? Stay out of our marriage?* She was, after all, fairly certain that Calisto didn't have a good side to which she could appeal.

Calisto raked her imperious gaze over Billie from her head to her toes and with a contemptuous toss of her head made it clear that she could not see what the source of her attraction was. 'Alexei and I were in love. You stole him from me. Did you really think it was going to be that simple? He's a Drakos and you're just a little office girl who got herself knocked up—oh, yes, I *know* about the kid,' she confirmed as she saw Billie's eyes widen in surprise.

'Alexei and I are married,' Billie heard herself say rather desperately, for she could think of no stronger verbal comeback.

Calisto just laughed again, a six-foot-tall

Amazonian blonde of spectacular beauty and shining confidence. 'That may be so but it doesn't change the fact that Alexei is my lover—'

'Alexei broke off your engagement,' Billie reminded her, struggling not to flinch at that bold claim that pierced her heart like a knife.

'He got cold feet—you must know the feeling well. After all, he abandoned you within hours of the big wedding. The press had a ball with that little detail, didn't they?' Calisto sniped with her perfect white-toothed smile. 'Alexei was on the rebound. He and I belong together but I should really thank you for having the all-important son and heir for me…'

'Thank me?' Billie frowned in bewilderment. 'What on earth are you trying to say?'

'That I'm not remotely kiddy-minded or interested in the idea of breeding babies, but that Alexei would have insisted that I have at least one child. I'm quite happy for that child to be *your* child. I'm not into stretch marks and saggy bits. I'm very proud of my perfect body. I'll be much happier as a stepmother than I would ever have been as a mother.'

'There is no way that I will ever let you near my son!' Billie snapped back in shaken retaliation, anger surging through her in a sudden adrenalin rush.

'Famous last words—do you really think that Alexei will give you a choice?' Calisto purred in a poisonously sweet response. 'He's very taken with the kid, isn't he? The next generation of the family dynasty and all that...when he divorces you, you'll be very lucky if he lets you keep custody of him.'

'Nobody is going to take my son away from me!' Billie shot back shakily and, whirling on her heel, she sped back to the front door because she recognised that the confrontation had gone beyond the stage where she could hold her own. She had also learned what she would rather not have known: Calisto knew way too much about Alexei and Billie's marriage, and about Nicky, whose very existence and paternity Billie had fondly imagined was still a secret known to only a precious few off the island of Speros.

Indeed the level of Calisto's information told Billie first and foremost that the gorgeous blonde enjoyed Alexei's complete trust. Clearly, Alexei had returned to his former lover as soon as he'd become disillusioned with his marriage, Billie registered sickly. He had to be sleeping with the Greek fashion model again.

Jealousy and despair assailed Billie in a dizzy wave. He had already discussed Nicky with Calisto, yet he had only found out that Nicky was his son early the day before. That Calisto should already know so much was uniquely revealing and her assurance in speaking as though she was to be Alexei's next wife was even more menacing.

As Billie walked with a down-bent head along the pavement to hide the tears spattering her cheeks in the fading light of evening a man straightened from the railings he had been leaning against and signalled the driver of the car parked further down the road. 'Kyria Drakos?'

Billie was shocked to recognise that it was Helios, the head of Alexei's security team, standing in her path. 'Helios?' she queried with a frown of surprise.

'Your husband asked me to collect you and convey you to the airport,' the older man told her with a caution that warned her that Helios was well aware of her obstinacy over her personal security at Hazlehurst earlier that morning and of Alexei's anger at her behaviour.

In a daze after her upsetting encounter with Calisto and truly appalled by the suspicion that Alexei might already be aware that she had tackled his former girlfriend, Billie climbed into the waiting limousine. While the luxurious vehicle struggled through the traffic she wondered how on earth her movements had been tracked all the way to her destination in Paris. She laid her mobile phone on the seat beside her and waited for Alexei to ring her with a heart sinking like a stone but it stayed mercifully silent. Her heart was hammering with nervous stress, her skin clammy with perspiration.

Had Alexei and Calisto already discussed future living arrangements for Nicky? It had sounded to her very much as though they had and her courage was failing her in the face of such a cruel, unfeeling threat to her love for her child. She felt sick and scared, while she inexorably recalled all the many times that she had stood back and watched while Alexei utilised every ruthless, clever and unemotional Drakos gene to come out on top. He was remorseless, determined to win every battle.

Helios took her to a private room at the airport and plied her tirelessly with magazines and refreshments as if he sensed her growing feeling of terror at her predicament. How could she be scared of Alexei? But she had never crossed him before to such an extent. It shook her that he had had her tracked down and retrieved like a wayward child even though she was in a foreign country. But in truth her own behaviour shook her even more. In one catastrophic move in facing up to Calisto she had fallen off the straight, narrow and sensible path she usually followed. But she had *needed* to know about Calisto, had needed to know that there were genuine grounds for her self-humiliating suspicions. She freshened up in the cloakroom, studying the pale drawn triangle of her face and seeing only Calisto's glowing physical beauty superimposed over her own. There was no contest; never had been and never would be.

Helios told her when it was time to board her flight home. 'Where is Alexei?' she could not help asking, for she had spent over an hour in that silent room, flinching every time she heard footsteps in the passage outside.

'Already on board,' the older man confirmed.

Shivering a little in the cool of late evening, Billie mounted the steps to the private jet and looked straight past the assembled flight crew greeting her to see Alexei seated with his laptop at a desk. The instant he saw her he lifted his arrogant dark head and vaulted upright. Blazing golden eyes struck hers and she almost reeled back from the force of the corrosive anger he was struggling to contain while they still had an audience. Walking down the aisle between the cream leather seating towards him felt as dangerous and daunting as walking a pirate's plank above shark-infested seas.

CHAPTER SEVEN

THE thrumming power of the jet as it took off sent vibrations rippling through Billie's taut slender length. As soon as they were airborne the crew served drinks and snacks, after which Alexei dismissed them. As the tension in the atmosphere took on an explosive edge, Billie gnawed at the soft underside of her lip until she could no longer bear the silence.

'What were you doing in Paris today?' she demanded thinly.

'The Drakos foundation was staging a charitable lunch,' Alexei answered, referring to the global charity set up by his father. 'I had a speech to make.'

She had a vague recollection of the luncheon benefit and compressed her lips. 'How did you know where I was?' she asked tautly.

'Helios only tracked you down when you arrived at the airport for your flight out to Paris.' Alexei's cool, controlled diction unnerved her and merely increased her wariness. 'So where did you go in London beforehand and who were you meeting? You were very keen to ensure that there were no witnesses.'

Billie turned her head and finally focused on him. 'I didn't want you to know that I was planning a trip to Paris as well,' she admitted baldly. 'I had no other motive and no reason to hide where I was going or what I was doing. Actually, I had my first meeting in London with my father over lunch today—'

That announcement certainly did grab Alexei's attention and his expressive brows drew together. 'Your father?' he exclaimed in disbelief. 'But I thought you had no idea who he was!'

Billie dug into her bag to retrieve the letter Desmond had written and leant across the aisle to pass it to Alexei.

His bold bronzed profile set hard while he scanned the comparatively brief communication.

'And until now you never even thought to mention this man's approach to me?' he ground out.

Billie reddened, for he sounded so astonished that she could have neglected to share the contents of that letter with him sooner. 'There was so much else going on between us at the time—'

'But you still just went ahead and arranged to meet this guy, taking him on trust?' Alexei thundered in interruption, springing upright to stare down at her in frank disbelief. 'You didn't even have a background check done on him! Have you any idea what a risk you took?'

'There was no risk,' Billie disclaimed. 'Desmond is a perfectly ordinary middle-aged businessman.'

'But this letter could have been a con trick to lure you into a vulnerable position.' His striking cheekbones prominent below his dark skin, golden eyes blistering, Alexei slowly shook his handsome head in angry wonderment. 'You could've been kidnapped, robbed, *anything*!' he spelt out angrily.

'Don't be so melodramatic—'

'Don't be so stupid,' Alexei retaliated with icy bite. 'You're part of my world now and worth more money as my wife than most people could earn in a lifetime. People maim and kill others for a great deal less. Round-the-clock protection is a necessary precaution to ensure your safety.'

A good deal paler than she had been after receiving that graphic warning, Billie nodded acceptance of his concern, which did ironically have the side effect of briefly lifting her mood. Alexei could be so cold and unemotional that it was good to know he cared enough to worry about her well-being to this extent. 'I promise that I won't be so trusting with anyone again, but my father is a very agreeable man.'

'That doesn't mean that he couldn't also be a fraudster on the make,' Alexei proclaimed with crushing cynicism. 'I'll have him thoroughly checked out before you see him again.'

Quietly convinced that her father was exactly who and what he purported to be, Billie made no comment. It struck her as deeply sad that she had had to look to Alexei's anger to find solace in the idea that he cared about what happened to her. Had their relationship always been so one-sided, so empty? Then he did not reciprocate her feelings, nor had he ever pretended to. She sipped her cold drink to moisten her dry mouth. 'Please don't let's talk about what I was doing in Paris,' she urged him in hasty appeal.

'How can I ignore what you did? What the hell were you thinking of when you went there?' Alexei responded with censorious golden eyes. 'You're my wife. I expect you to behave with dignity. That does not mean confronting Calisto in one of our homes and accusing her of having an affair with me.'

Her face burning at that rebuke, Billie lifted her chin. 'I wasn't sure that you still regarded me as your wife. Most of our conversations since our wedding have ended with you walking out or talking about us being over as a couple...'

Golden eyes gleaming, Alexei loosed a harsh laugh of challenge. 'You make me sound *so* unreasonable. Nobody would credit that you spent more than a year lying to me and then produced my son like a rabbit out of a magician's hat the same day that I married you!'

Having paled at that accurate if acerbic summing-up of her sins, Billie swallowed hard. She registered that in his eyes she was never going to live down her past and concentrated on what mattered most to her at that moment. 'I'm still entitled to ask you what's going on between you and Calisto.'

'Nothing sexually.' Alexei's wide sensual mouth took on a sardonic twist. 'It's business now. Her father died during our relationship and in his will he placed me in charge of her inheritance. As she was one of three children the legacy was not particularly large. But when I parted from Calisto it was on poor terms and it was easier for me to ignore the responsibility her father had given me. While I was doing that, she got into considerable debt.'

'*Debt?*' Billie leant forward to question in un-abashed surprise at that statement. 'I thought

Calisto was a wealthy woman in her own right.'

'So did she, but she didn't get a big divorce settlement because of the pre-nuptial agreement she signed with Bethune,' Alexei informed her wryly. 'And as the wife and then the girlfriend of two very rich men there was never any need for her to watch her expenditure. But once she was living on her own income, she quickly got into trouble.'

'And because of this, she's now living in your town house in Paris?' Billie had already worked out the direction his cool explanation was going in and she was not overly impressed by it. So, poor Calisto had finally been forced to live as an independent woman and settle her own bills! She could see that such an obligation would have been uncomfortable for Alexei in the aftermath of a broken relationship, but she did not accept the need for him to have got involved again with Calisto on such a very personal basis. He could easily have brought in an accountant or lawyer to take charge of the

Greek woman's financial affairs and have kept Calisto at arm's length.

'If I had done my duty by Calisto as her late father expected of me, her finances would never have got in such a mess,' Alexei reasoned as if his involvement and sense of guilt were the most natural and understandable reactions in the world. 'As she's currently working for a Parisian fashion house, it made sense for her to use my property as a base and reduce her outgoings.'

Billie wondered why he hadn't just settled his ex-fiancée's debts in compensation for his neglect of her affairs. Billie could not help thinking about the amount of very private information about their marriage that Calisto had apparently had full access to and she reckoned that she was only receiving part of the truth from her volatile husband. Alexei and his former lover were clearly on very close terms again. It was possible that that intimacy had not yet stretched to accommodate a renewed sexual relationship, but it could only be a matter of time until it did. Perhaps Calisto was also being given a second chance to prove herself and Alexei was biding his time before reaching any firm decision about his future plans. After all, he had dived at un-characteristic speed into their marriage and what had that gained him? A son she'd dragged like a rabbit out of a magician's hat?

'You shouldn't have gone anywhere near Calisto,' Alexei breathed grimly, his hard gaze cutting into her like a laser beam. 'Today, when you subjected her to a jealous scene, you embar-rassed me. I expect more from you than that kind of gutter behaviour.'

While inwardly cringing at that rebuke, Billie perfectly understood how Calisto had deliv-ered her into Alexei's hands, gift-wrapped and tagged, and as a jealous vengeful witch. Calisto must have got onto the phone within minutes of Billie's departure to get her version of events in first. Alexei believed she had gone to fight over him with another woman and, as she had never really known how she planned to tackle Calisto or indeed what she would say to her, she could not have come up with a more dignified explanation for her visit.

Alexei surveyed her steadily, lush black lashes screening his gaze to the hot gleaming gold of a hunting animal, while his dark accented drawl took on a husky deep note that shimmied down her sensitive spine like a caress. 'Before today, I would never have dreamt that you would act in such a primitive way, *moraki mou*. I've always admired your restraint and intelligence.'

'Well, it just goes to show that you never really know anyone,' Billie quipped unevenly, marvelling at the stunning beauty and power of his eyes and feeling her treacherous body quicken in a physical response as natural to her in his presence as the feel of her own skin. Her nipples peaking into straining buds, she wondered whether she should shout at him for calling her 'primitive' or revel in his evident fascination because something equally basic in him clearly liked the idea of her fighting for him. And nothing had ever illustrated for her so clearly the innate dichotomy of Alexei Drakos the man, censuring her behaviour while reserving the right to sexually savour it.

Billie closed her eyes tight on temptation. And he was the ultimate temptation for her and always had been. But the time for that kind of behaviour was past, she told herself firmly, crushing the inner quivers of desire that would have destroyed her self-respect had she let them linger. Unlike him she refused to take refuge in sex when their relationship was falling apart and she could not accept his current intimacy with Calisto Bethune either.

Maybe he hadn't yet got back into bed with his ex-fiancée but that did not make his betrayal of their marriage any easier to bear. He had shared *their* secrets and evidently even discussed who would get custody of their son. She could not forgive him for that disloyalty. He had been right on one score though. Until she had spoken to Calisto, Billie would have fought for their marriage with whatever weapons came to hand. But loving Alexei was no longer enough and she *had* made some terrible mistakes, she acknowledged painfully. Now, however, she felt alienated and on the brink of being discarded, a humiliating sensation that did not sit well with her pride. It was really time for her to look out for her own interests and those of her son and prepare for a future that did not include Alexei. Furthermore, rather than wait to be pushed she was discovering that she would very much prefer to jump.

'Billie…' Alexei murmured thickly.

'No, don't look at me that way, don't talk to me that way either,' she told him tautly. 'It's no longer appropriate.'

Alexei frowned at her evasive eyes and cool intonation, the sensual heat dying out of his intent gaze. 'What are you talking about?'

Billie breathed in deep. 'Marrying you without telling you about Nicky was a huge mistake,' she admitted heavily, lifting her head to study her husband with pained eyes. 'But fortunately we don't have to live with that mistake for ever.'

Alexei had fallen very still. 'Meaning?'

'You were right. We should get a divorce,' she extended flatly, pinning her tremulous lip line firm as she voiced that ground-breaking decision.

'I only entertained that idea *before* I knew we had a child!' Alexei raked back at her with disdainful force. 'Now that I do know, a divorce is out of the question.'

'But we're not working out as a couple.'

'And whose fault is that?' Alexei raked back at her.

'It's not *all* my fault,' Billie told him, green eyes flaming back at him like highly polished jewels. 'Your renewed intimacy with Calisto—'

'There *is* no intimacy!' Alexei broke in angrily.

Billie gave him a stony look. 'Well, there's a closeness that I find unacceptable.'

'You find it…unacceptable?' Alexei framed in a raw undertone of wrath.

'As you said, trust is gone,' Billie reminded him tightly. 'Calisto was a major part of your life for many months while I was pregnant and I refuse to stand by on the sidelines again while you entertain her.'

Black-lashed bronzed eyes brilliant with fury at her daring to lay down the law to him, Alexei spread his arms wide in an angry movement of dismissal. 'You are my wife,' he growled between compressed lips. 'That should be enough for you.'

'But it's not enough. I feel like an accidental wife, not a real one. You said I cheated you. You regretted marrying me within hours of the ceremony.' While Billie grimaced, she also held her head high as she reminded him of those facts. 'I can't rewrite our past and neither can you.'

A screaming silence that flared along the edges like an inflamed wound fell in the opulent cabin.

'I won't give you a divorce,' Alexei delivered in sardonic challenge.

'I don't mind waiting a bit longer to get the legal stuff over and done with,' she said wearily, a thumping headache beginning to pound behind her temples. 'But while you can hold things up you can't stop me getting a divorce. I know enough about the law to know that.'

Bronzed eyes shimmering like polished metal, Alexei set his even white teeth together.

Billie sensed his brooding dark fury and watched his long brown fingers tighten to show the white of bone round the glass in his hand. He was a Drakos, an Alpha male with a very powerful personality, and he was outraged that *she* should talk of divorcing *him* when he blamed her for the disintegration of their marriage. She understood that, she understood that perfectly, but she was fed up of eating humble pie, turning the other cheek and staying quiet when she wanted to demand answers and felt she deserved more understanding. As yet she could not even imagine a life without Alexei in it, but in time she would get stronger and she would get over him...*oh, yes, she would!* She had more than enough strength and resolve and courage, she told herself fiercely.

A barrage of paparazzi awaited them at Heathrow Airport. Cameras flashed to catch the first sight of Alexei Drakos together with his English-born wife since a single official wedding photo had been released. Questions were shouted and, certain someone had asked her about her child, Billie shied away, wondering if Nicky's existence had now become public knowledge. Alexei stopped dead so suddenly that she almost tripped over him.

'I have a son,' he announced with considerable pride and satisfaction. 'His name is Nikolos.'

And with that Alexei turned to close an arm round Billie and herd her onward out of the airport. 'You might have warned me that you were planning to do that!' she exclaimed.

'It had to be done,' Alexei fielded without a shade of apology. 'I will not tolerate speculation about my son's paternity when a simple acknowledgement from me will protect both you and him from spurious rumours.'

So, now everyone would think that Nicky was the reason why Alexei had married her. He had laid bare the fact to the world that she had conceived his son before he had even got together with Calisto Bethune. His relations would be shocked, but then they were very well used to being shocked by Alexei and would probably honour him for marrying the mother of his firstborn son, just as his father had once done a generation ago. Billie asked herself why she should still be so sensitive to those facts when she had already reached the decision that their relationship had no future. Obviously she needed to grow a much tougher skin.

'We'll fly back to the island tomorrow,' Alexei told her smoothly as she slid into the waiting limousine.

Billie turned startled eyes on him and he closed a hand over hers. 'No...' she began.

'You can't run out on our marriage after three weeks,' Alexei drawled with a soft sure sibilance that filled her with disquiet.

'Why shouldn't I?' Billie dealt him a defiant glance and snatched her hand free of his. Sometimes she thought she had spent half her life waiting for Alexei to return after he had walked away from her. As an employee madly in love with her boss, she had been defenceless. Even when pregnant with his baby she had contrived to be powerless because she had not stood up for her rights. She had been too sensitive, too proud to face her fear of being a burden and an embarrassment to him. But her days of martyrdom and victimhood were now at an end. This time around she would do what was right for her and what suited Alexei wasn't going to influence her, she promised herself, having stoked up her anger with him to a fine burning heat.

'As for me running out on our marriage, *you* didn't even last the length of our wedding night,' Billie completed in provocative addition.

'That is past. We're not children. Indeed, we have a child to consider. We have to work this out,' Alexei informed her grittily.

'I've already worked out what is best for me and I'm not going back to live on *your* island, to stay in *your* house to be surrounded by *your* people!' Billie rounded on him to respond with ferocious resolve.

'What has got into you?' Alexei bit out with a roughened edge of incredulity in his dark deep accented voice.

Staring out of the windows at the dark lamp-lit streets of the city and the ever-present surge of traffic, Billie dropped her head to study the hands she had linked together on her lap. 'I'm thinking of me for a change, not of you.'

'Try thinking about our son instead. He would be more relevant.'

'No, don't you dare try that maternal guilt trip on me!' Billie flared back at him in furious rebuttal, her small face stiff with resentment. 'You seduced me, you got me pregnant, then you conveniently lost your memory. I did the best I could for my child in a rotten situation and I don't owe anyone anything, least of all you!'

Bemused by the positive violence of her response, Alexei studied her fixedly, his bold bronzed profile taut, his piercing gaze assessing her hectically flushed face. 'Forget about me. I'm actually asking you to put the needs of our son first.'

Billie flung up a hand in a silencing motion, angry that he could dare to attack her on that front. 'I've made enough sacrifices and

I'm not in the mood to make any more!' she warned him.

'You're being totally irrational. Only today you flew over to Paris to confront Calisto—that's not the behaviour of a woman who wants a divorce.'

Billie glued her lips together in a mutinous line. As far as she was concerned taking part in any further discussion concerning Calisto would be humiliating for her and she had no intention of going there.

'I want a divorce,' she repeated steadily. 'I want my life back and my new life will naturally be here in England.'

'Is that a fact?' Alexei interposed with a scantily leashed savagery of tone that made her turn back to stare at him.

'Well, why would I want to live on Speros any longer? At least I can get a job here,' she pointed out squarely.

'You're talking about taking my child away from me as if it means nothing,' Alexei condemned in an aggressive undertone.

'But we can't stay married just for Nicky's

sake,' Billie protested helplessly. 'I want more, I *need* more than some empty charade of a relationship. I'm not prepared to spend the rest of my life paying for the mistake I made on the night of the funeral.'

'If you live in England, I will see very little of our son. I consider my role in his life to be as important as yours. You're being unreasonable and unfair. Nikolos needs both of us.'

Billie could hear his continuing surprise at the way she was behaving and she wondered why he expected her to be reasonable when he had been so very judgemental and inflexible since she had fallen off her pedestal with a crash on their wedding night. Right at that moment, after enduring all the stresses and strains of an inordinately long and eventful day, she was at the end of her tether. She was too tired to argue with him, for he would keep up the pressure and refuse to quit until he wore her opinions down and she knew that she could not afford to allow that to happen this time around.

It would be a ghastly joke to divorce Alexei

and end up living as his ex-wife on the island of Speros. What life would she have there? Once again she would be living on the edge of *his* life, watching him with Calisto or some other woman, and for the sake of her sanity she just couldn't *do* that any more! A fresh start far away from Alexei and his influence was what she needed, not a rehash of the past when constant exposure to him had enslaved her and ruined her for any other man. So as far as where she lived was concerned she was fully convinced that she had no choice but to be unreasonable as he called it.

A huge weariness that encompassed Billie's entire body was gaining on her steadily. She let her heavy eyelids slide shut and thought longingly of having Nicky in her arms again. The love of her child would surely fill the giant black hole where her heart used to be. Without Alexei around to upset and distract her, she would be able to concentrate on being a mother. That thought was the very last thought she would later remember.

* * *

Billie woke up slowly the next morning. It was just after eight and a twinge of guilt assailed her because Kasma would already have given Nicky his morning feed. The pillow beside hers was pristine and untouched and she knew that once again she had slept alone. Alexei had put her to bed in her unexciting white cotton underwear. She wondered with a sudden savage pain if he had smiled when he saw what she wore underneath her clothes and recalled her warning on that wedding night that had gone so terribly wrong. No, Alexei had probably not been any more in the mood to smile the night before than she had been, she acknowledged unhappily, sliding out of bed and heading into the bathroom for a quick shower.

In fact Alexei, she conceded ruefully, was much more concerned for Nicky's future in the event of a divorce than she would ever have believed. His own parents, of course, had maintained a stable relationship, setting their only a child a good example. She pictured Alexei as she had seen him with Nicky only two days earlier, their son lying trustingly asleep in his father's arms. Alexei had proved to be much more hands-on with his son than she had expected as well. Indeed he had accepted Nicky straight away and had immediately wanted to get to know their child.

Of course she recognised the importance of a father in her son's life! She wasn't stupid, nor was she so selfish that she wanted to keep Nicky all to herself. She would make every reasonable effort to share their son with Alexei, but he was primarily based in Greece and she was not prepared to continue living abroad for his benefit. Was that so heinous a crime?

As Billie got dressed she was still rationalising the decisions she had reached the day before. Alexei no longer respected or trusted her. They had no relationship left to save. A quick divorce would be a better solution to their predicament than a long dragged-out marital breakdown. Why shouldn't Alexei spend more time in London? Was that so much to ask of him? Surely they could both be good and effective parents even if they lived far apart?

Still stressing about the serious conclusions she had made after the trip to Paris, Billie went up the flight of stairs to the nursery, which was traditionally and inconveniently sited on the top floor of the house. She walked into the room, which was empty, and crossed it to knock on the door of the bedroom that Kasma was using. When there was no answer she opened the door. There was no sign of Nicky's nurse or of her belongings. Indeed the bed had been stripped. Her brow furrowing, Billie went back out onto the landing. The housekeeper was emerging from her self-contained flat on the other side of the gallery.

'Did Kasma take Nicky out for a walk?' Billie asked the older woman.

The housekeeper looked surprised at the question. 'Mr Drakos flew out at dawn with Kasma and the little boy…' Her voice faltered as Billie went white and closed her hands tight round the stair rail. 'Is there anything wrong, Mrs Drakos?'

Billie didn't know what she said, but afterwards

she went back into the empty nursery to get a grip on herself and on the shocking news that Alexei had simply taken their son out of the country with him without her permission. She looked down into the cot and finally noticed that, strangely, her mobile phone was lying on top of the disturbed bedding. She lifted it and registered that it was flashing because it had an unopened message.

'Call me,' ran the text, and it was from Alexei. He must have deliberately placed the phone there for her to find it.

Call him? She wanted to throw the mobile through the unopened window, tear the room apart and scream her fury loud enough to be heard in Greece! Call him? She was so shattered by what he had done that she could barely think straight. He had kidnapped Nicky and taken him abroad without her knowledge, indeed knowing that she had other plans. How dared he? *How flipping dared he?* Denied her son when her arms ached for him, Billie was overwhelmed by the sudden fear that Alexei was already making a bid for custody of their child. Her heart seemed to skip a beat and she felt sick as she pelted downstairs to check her handbag for Nicky's passport. As she had expected, it had gone.

CHAPTER EIGHT

'What the hell have you done?' Billie yelled down the phone the minute her call was answered. 'Where is Nicky?'

'Here at our house in the South of France with me. He's about to have lunch. He's fine.'

That Alexei and her son were in France took Billie aback and she could only dimly assume that there was some advantage to that location that she had yet to work out. 'You kidnapped him…how could you do that to me?'

'My jet is waiting at Heathrow for you. I'm sure it won't take you long to pack,' Alexei countered without remorse.

Barely able to vocalise, never mind think, Billie was trembling with rage and distress. 'If you were standing here in front of me, I honestly believe I would kill you!' she hissed at him and she flung the phone down on her bed, folded her arms and stared at it with rampant loathing.

Arrogantly ignoring everything she had said the previous day, indeed clearly impervious to her wishes, her opinions *and* her feelings, Alexei had removed his son from his mother's care and taken him to another country. It was a shocking move that filled Billie to overflowing with dark, fearful foreboding for the future. As a gesture it was uniquely effective, for in that one outrageous act of aggression Alexei had contrived to jerk all her strings at once as though she were nothing but a puppet he was able to control.

Billie was truly shattered. It honestly had not occurred to her that Alexei might fight dirty from the word go. She had assumed they could be civilised—at least in the initial stages of a separation. She had most definitely not been prepared for a war in which no holds were barred to break out so fast. Why had Alexei taken their son to France? Was there some legal advantage in doing this? For the first time in her life Billie regretted not following her mother's guidance and approaching a divorce lawyer. In business, Alexei always took keen advantage of legal advice and she was convinced that Alexei would have sought a professional opinion of what he had just done before he did it. She wished she could have grabbed at the comfort of believing that he was too stupid to appreciate that such behaviour might be held against him in a divorce court when it came to discussing his access to their son. But having worked for Alexei for so long and seeing at first hand how in touch with events and boundaries he always was, she could find no consolation in that line of thought.

Dressed in a yellow shift dress, Billie watched her luggage being stowed in the silver SUV that had come to collect her from the flight to Nice. The sun was warmer and brighter than it had been at Hazlehurst and the sky was a great bright arc of endless blue above her head. Alexei's idyllic chateau in the unspoilt Luberon Valley had always been her favourite Drakos property so it struck her as especially ironic that he should have taken Nicky there. As they travelled deeper into the countryside hills the colour of ochre gave a dramatic edge to the scenery and fields of purple lavender stretched as far as the horizon. Stands of woodland, peach orchards and the serried ranks of highly productive vines that belonged to the chateau surrounded the little medieval settlement of Claudel that was perched high on a rocky cliff like so many other fortified villages in the area. On the uphill climb the SUV traversed the narrow streets with care, snaking across the sleepy village square past the beautiful old church to take a steep cobbled lane lined with medieval dwellings and terminated by the elaborate turreted entrance to the chateau. The electronic gates whirred shut in the vehicle's wake.

In front of the ancient stone bulk of the chateau, which had, over the years, been burned down and ruined many times only to be rebuilt to survive another century, Billie sprang out of the car. She didn't take the time to admire the magnificent view of the village and the valley below and she paid no heed at all to the lovely peaceful

gardens where she had so often sat basking in
the sunshine. Indeed she barely paused to greet
the maid who opened the solid oak front door,
and sped down a corridor walled with rough
stone to thrust open the door of the room Alexei
used as an office…and there he was: her quarry!
Impervious to the warmth of the day in the air-
conditioned room, he was very elegantly clad
in a dark blue designer suit fashionably cut to
define every sexy, virile line of his long powerful thighs, muscular chest and broad shoulders.
Her heartbeat kicked up speed, her breathing
straining in her throat. She hated his guts like
poison at that moment but there was no denying
that he was gorgeous.

Alexei surveyed her with glittering golden eyes
and there was neither apology nor remorse in
that bold challenging appraisal. 'No shouting,'
he warned her.

But Billie was so violently angry to discover
that he had relaxed and simply got on with working while she agonised over the disappearance of
her son that she sought the nearest heavy object,

swept it off the side table and threw it at him with all her strength. Alexei ducked in the nick of time and the metal paperweight she had lifted sailed over his shoulder and smashed through the window behind him.

Just a little shaken by the hail of broken glass noisily showering the floor, which Alexei hastily stepped back from, Billie breathed bitterly, 'I wish I'd hit you.'

'Mercifully you missed—your French isn't good enough to handle a murder charge in a court here, *mali mou*,' Alexei quipped, and as the door burst loudly open to frame an anxious Helios he smiled and dismissed his bodyguard with a fluid movement of a lean brown hand. 'An accident, Helios. My apologies for disturbing you.'

Billie set her teeth together so hard she was surprised they didn't splinter. 'I don't have the words to tell you what I think of you. Have you any idea how I felt when I learned that you had taken Nicky abroad? Do you know what it felt like when I saw that empty cot?' she launched at him in a shaking voice of rage once Helios had withdrawn again. 'He's my son and you had no right to take him away from me.'

Alexei rested steady dark golden eyes on her angry troubled face. 'Yet you were prepared to do the exact same thing to me,' he said silkily.

For a split second Billie was transfixed by that unexpected comeback. 'You can't compare my choosing to live in England to what you did today!'

'Can't I?' A well-shaped black brow lifted. 'Speaking as someone who knows my commitments as well as I do, how often do you think I was going to get to see my son?'

Billie lost colour and compressed her lips, refusing to be drawn on that score.

'But you were quite happy to impose that loss on me,' Alexei declared with a raw edge to his deep voice. 'And do you know why? You've spent the past five months ignoring my rights as a father and you see no reason why that can't continue.'

'You're twisting things—I'm not that selfish!' Billie protested.

'You are where our son is concerned,' Alexei contradicted in Greek. 'And that's why I took him today, knowing that you would follow us.'

'Never in my life have I heard anything more reckless or irresponsible!' Billie fired back at him furiously. 'I was so scared when I realised you'd taken him…it was wicked and unpardonable to put me through that.'

'You knew he would come to no harm in my care and Kasma's. I would consider it equally wicked were you to deprive our son of his father,' Alexei drawled with a steely sibilance that cut through her defences.

'Message received!' Billie flung back at him angrily, her complexion reddening. 'But you didn't have to go to such lengths to make your point!'

'Didn't I?' Alexei replied, unimpressed. 'You're even more stubborn than I am when you get the bit between your teeth.'

'What you did was *wrong*.'

'I agree, but you didn't give me a choice,' Alexei reasoned, having astonished her with that initial admission of fault. 'I have no intention of being an occasional father. Our son will need my guidance as a child and as an adult, and if we don't forge a close relationship now you can kiss goodbye to me having any influence with him when he's older.'

For just a moment, Billie recalled how wild Alexei had been as an adolescent, with unlimited wealth and two very indulgent parents. Constantine Drakos had only ever interfered in Alexei's life when he believed his son might be in physical danger. It dawned on Billie that one day Nicky might be just as rich, wilful and careless of his own safety as Alexei had once been, and when that day came it very probably would take a personality as forceful as Alexei's to exercise control over their son.

Billie stiffened. 'I *do* appreciate that you have an important role in Nicky's life as well.'

'But until this moment you weren't prepared to make any allowances for the fact.'

The pink tip of her tongue slid out to moisten her dry lower lip. She was beginning to feel like someone pinned between a rock and a hard place. 'Maybe I was a little hasty in some of the things I decided.'

Lush ebony lashes fanned down low on his electrifying golden gaze, and as he stared at the glistening curve of her voluptuous lower lip a nerve ending pulled taut in her pelvis. She shifted uneasily off one foot onto the other. Alexei strolled towards her as lithe as a hunting cat on the prowl. The atmosphere hummed with sexual awareness and she fought her responses with all her might. Alexei made no such attempt, closing his hands to her hips to urge her close. As she parted her lips to object he brought his sensual mouth down hungrily on hers, his tongue delving into the tender interior between her lips with an erotic heat that made every nerve ending in her treacherous body sit up and take notice. A trembling started low down inside her, her bra constricting her swelling breasts, a snaking burn and surge of moisture tingling between her thighs. And in that fiery instant she learned that she could hate Alexei but still want him with a remorseless, bone-deep craving that was terrifyingly strong.

'*No!*' she told him fierily, striking her fist against a broad hard shoulder and when he didn't immediately draw back doing so again.

He lifted his arrogant dark head. His bronzed gaze burned her like honey heated to boiling point, unbearably sweet and tempting. 'Even if it's what we both want, *glyka mou*?'

Billie threw back her head, jewelled green eyes bright as rapier blades. 'I don't do *just* sex, Alexei. You should know that by now.'

'You have impossible standards.'

'Only to someone like you.' Deep inside, she was squashing a wealth of pain and regret that it should be that way. She didn't do just sex but he didn't do love or for ever and, even worse, she wasn't even sure that he knew *how* to do them. For a little while she had assumed he loved Calisto, but nobody witnessing the smooth, unemotional way he had moved on from that affair could have believed that he was nursing a broken heart. If he had decided that he wanted Calisto back, it was most probably because she suited him and his lifestyle better than Billie could.

'I've always enjoyed a challenge,' Alexei riposted, a strong hand on her spine trying to urge her back into his arms.

'Right now, I just want to see my son,' Billie announced, hectic colour in her face but sincerity shining in her clear gaze.

And the darkening of Alexei's beautiful eyes, the tensing of his stunning dark features, would have signified annoyance had she been naïve enough to believe that his responses could be that human. He freed her, thrust open the door and escorted her in silence up the sweeping staircase, which would have looked more at home in an antebellum mansion than in a hilltop chateau with the core of a medieval fortress. But then it was exactly that endearing quirkiness that she had always loved about the Chateau Claudel. Each new owner had added personal touches, few of which were historically accurate.

Nicky was lying in his cot, Kasma busy tidying away toys. As Anatalya's daughter moved to greet her Billie recognised the relief the younger woman couldn't hide and knew that Kasma had been uneasy about her charge's removal from his mother's care. Her son kicked up his bare toes and gave her a wide gummy smile, which told her that while her world might have been rocked on its axis, all was right in his. Her heart beating very fast, Billie reached down into the cot and scooped the baby up, loving the weight of him in her arms and the sweet familiar smell of his skin as she cuddled him close. Alexei was watching and she gave him a fierce warning look before she gave her attention back to the child she adored.

'Where are you going?' he enquired as she headed for the stairs.

'I think I'll sit in the garden for a while… before I pack his things,' she tacked on as casually as she could, for she refused to reward Alexei's cruel manipulation of her attachment to her child by staying on in France.

His lean dark face shadowed, dense ebony lashes fanning down on his stunning eyes as he absorbed that unapologetic statement. 'I can't let you do that,' he murmured very softly, but she was not taken in by that softness of tone because she knew that the cooler and the quieter Alexei was, the more dangerous he was.

She didn't reply. She walked with Nicky in her arms outside into the afternoon heat and sought the bench in the shade of the ancient oak tree in the walled garden. There she had often sat to enjoy the magnificent view. *I can't let you do that*. Did he mean to physically prevent her from leaving with Nicky? Or was he planning to flex his muscles in some other way?

'Your father is so, *so* tricky,' she sighed into her son's tousled black hair.

The tranquillity of the garden and the silence enclosed her, soothing her anxious thoughts. But she could not escape her recollection of her dialogue with Alexei. At first she had been so angry with him that she couldn't think, but then he had *made* her think of what her plans would mean to him. Regardless of what happened between them, she had never wanted to shut him out of his child's life or to damage their chances of develop-ing a normal father and son relationship. But she was only beginning to get used to the concept of sharing her son with his father and she knew that the concept of sharing anything was a worryingly alien concept to any Drakos male.

If she insisted on living in England she would be making it very difficult for Alexei to develop strong ties with his son. Yet the alternative of living on the island would cruelly restrict her life in every way and make it virtually impossible for her to move on as an independent woman. She supposed the bottom line ought to be what would most benefit her son, not herself. Perhaps there was no happy-medium solution that would be beneficial to both her and her son. But enabling Nicky to enjoy a close relationship with both his parents would be the wisest, kindest option, she acknowledged ruefully. It was just unfortunate that that might well have to come at the price of her freedom.

Hearing a step, she glanced up and saw Alexei with Kasma and a pushchair in tow. Nicky had drifted off to sleep and when the nursemaid offered to take him, Billie passed him over. As Kasma wheeled him away Billie glimpsed the momentarily tender and unfamiliar expression on Alexei's lean strong face as he gazed appreciatively down at his son and her heart stabbed her. Alexei, who had all his life been adored but who, as far as Billie was aware, had never truly responded to any woman after his mother, had somehow and in a very short space of time contrived to become deeply attached to his infant son.

'We have to talk,' Alexei delivered as soon as Kasma had headed back indoors with her charge.

Billie viewed his tall, powerful figure with pained eyes. 'You didn't need to steal him to make me understand how much he meant to you as well. You could just have told me.'

His hard jaw line clenched as if her candid reference to his obvious attachment to Nicky had embarrassed him. 'You weren't willing to listen.'

Billie didn't want to plunge them back into an argument by referring to all that had passed between them since their wedding. She had done wrong but so had he. Yet he was still the guy that she loved with all her heart, she acknowledged unhappily. No matter how angry or frustrated he made her, she never lost sight of what he meant to her. 'I was very shocked that you just took Nicky's passport and whisked him away from me,' she admitted tautly. 'What would you have done had I called in the police?'

Alexei froze, his lean powerful face washing clean of expression, his eyes glittering dark as night in the shade of the tree. 'I would have informed them that I have legal custody of my son.'

Her smooth brow indented. 'What the heck are you talking about?'

The blankness of his features was put to flight as he bit out a rare curse in Greek before saying, 'You didn't read the pre-nuptial agreement, did you? I couldn't credit you would be that trusting, but obviously you were…'

Billie leapt upright, all her attention locked to him. 'Why? What was in the agreement?'

'If you gave me a child you signed away all rights over that child to me.'

Billie stared back at him in disbelief, her flush in the heat of the day fading to be replaced by pallor. 'That's not possible.'

'Billie….' Alexei spread fluid brown hands in instinctive appeal to her natural intelligence '…when you only hire the very cleverest lawyers in the world, *anything* you want is possible.'

CHAPTER NINE

For the longest period of her life, Billie stared at Alexi in horror. 'But you didn't even know we had a child when we got married.'

'But I hoped there would be one eventually and, after my father's various costly excursions into matrimony, my legal team naturally sought to protect me against every possible threat in the future. If we break up, I retain custody of our children.'

Her legs wobbling, Billie slowly sank down on the bench again. 'I would never have knowingly signed such a contract. It's immoral. I trusted you and you cheated me…'

'There was no deception. You signed the document without reading it,' he pointed out drily. 'How wise was that?'

'You actually thought that I would be willing

to give up all rights over my own children just to marry you?'

Alexei shook his dark head with wry amusement. 'You know better than that. There are women in this world who would give their last pint of their blood to marry me.'

'Possibly not if they're sitting where I'm sitting,' Billie tacked on helplessly. 'Do you honestly think that something like that would stand up in court?'

'I don't want to take you to court. I don't want to remove my son from your care. I don't want a divorce either,' he completed with measured emphasis.

Billie got up again on knees that felt shaky. 'I wish I had never slept with you and never had your child. But my worst mistake was marrying you.'

'I'm grateful that you did all those things. I don't want to turn the clock back. I would very much like to remember the night our son was conceived—' Alexei sent her a gleaming glance of rampant curiosity that made her bridle '—but in the absence of that, I am delighted and proud to have a son.'

And he didn't want a divorce. Now she was beginning to wonder if she did either. In a divorce he might well exercise the legal right to take charge of their son and what would that do to her? Would he win if she fought him in a court? Was that a risk she was prepared to take? If she lost the right to be the primary carer of the child that she loved, what would her freedom be worth to her then? Her blood was already chilling in her veins at the very idea of such deprivation.

'You're blackmailing me,' she condemned in disgust.

'I want you to give our marriage a chance.' Alexei held her angry gaze with level cool and considerable force of will. 'That's why I took Nicky and why I brought you out here to join us. I was playing for bigger stakes than making some stupid point!'

'I don't like being manipulated and intimidated into doing what you want. I don't think the end justifies the means,' Billie argued forcefully. 'Do you want to know what you've really achieved? You've made me appreciate that I couldn't bear to stay married to someone like you!'

As Billie attempted to walk past him Alexei closed a hand like a steel cuff to her arm and held her back. 'I won't let you go.'

'I'm not giving you a choice!' she blazed back up at him, wrenching her arm violently free of his hold.

'What the hell has come over you?' Alexei bit out, staring down at her with hard questioning eyes. 'I'm willing to fight for you and our marriage. How is that blackmail? How is that something to be ashamed of? What's right and what's wrong doesn't come into this. You and Nikolos are my family now and I'm not going to lose you!'

Family. It was a word with very deep and important connotations for Billie. She had had an unhappy childhood and a difficult adolescence with a mother who was incapable of putting her child's needs before her own. She had grown up envying schoolmates with two parents, longing to be a part of family rituals like birthday parties and lunches when their whole families, young and old alike, would get together. She had always blithely assumed that some day she would create that family backdrop to nourish her own children's need for love, support and security. Now as an adult she was learning that life was not so simple and that being part of a family demanded personal sacrifices. Did she stay married to a man who didn't love her? Did she walk in eyes wide open and settle for that kind of marriage because it was the best she was likely to get and because she loved him?

Alexei surveyed her grimly as she settled back down on the bench, turning her face away from him and returning to studying the view.

'I feel like the real you is locked up inside, somewhere I can't reach you,' he admitted in a roughened undertone.

'It's only because I'm not behaving like an employee any longer,' Billie murmured ruefully. 'I'm standing up to you and you don't like it.'

'You always stood up to me,' Alexei contradicted.

Her mobile phone was buzzing like an angry wasp in her pocket and with a look of apology in Alexei's direction she pulled it out and moved away a few steps to answer it. It was Hilary, but her aunt was so upset and talking so fast that Billie had to beg her to calm down and talk more clearly.

'Mum's...*where*?' Billie pressed in dismay. 'Doing what?'

'It's too late, Billie. I'm upset on your behalf but there's nothing you can do. Lauren signed a contract, took the money and is now living it up in a London hotel. I don't know when the article will be published. And I think Lauren handed over photos of Nicky as well,' Hilary revealed unhappily. 'I'm so sorry. If I had had the slightest idea of what your mother was planning to do, I would've tried to dissuade her, but the first I knew of what she was up to was when she called me from London to boast about how rich and famous she was going to be!'

'What's wrong?' Alexei demanded, alerted by the consternation on Billie's face and the growing anger.

'This is not your problem, Hilary. Which hotel is she in?' Finally, Billie finished the call and turned back to Alexei. 'You're not going to believe what Mum's done—she's talked about us to some British Sunday newspaper and they've paid her a fortune for it. She's even given them private photographs of Nicky!' she exclaimed furiously.

'It was an accident waiting to happen.' Alexei shrugged a broad shoulder. 'I did consider paying her to keep quiet about us but I knew you would be annoyed if I intervened with that kind of an offer.'

'Why on earth should she be bribed to keep quiet? How could my mother *sell* pictures of her own grandson?' Billie gasped strickenly.

Alexei was a good deal less surprised by Lauren's perfidy than Billie was. Over the years several lovers, acquaintances and even minor relatives of his own had profited from selling stories about him and his family to the tabloid press. He had long appreciated that Lauren Foster would be vulnerable to such an approach.

'I'll have to go back to London to see her!' Billie announced, so angry with her scheming parent that she was trembling with the force of her feelings. Lauren's efforts to prevent her sister from finding out what she was planning to do proved that Billie's mother had known perfectly well that she was doing something very wrong.

'It won't change anything. If she signed a contract, what's done is done,' Alexei pronounced. 'Leave Nicky here. The press could well be lying in wait for you to visit.'

'Why aren't you furious?' Billie demanded with incomprehension.

'I've always had to live with media intrusion. That's why I like the privacy laws here in France. The paparazzi have to follow the rules here.'

Almost grateful to have to deal with a problem that did not relate to her marriage and its uncertain future, Billie went back into the house to change. It was ironic to discover that she didn't want to leave France or her son. Nevertheless, she did feel an overriding need to confront her mother because all too often in the past she had turned a blind eye to Lauren's greed and dishonesty for the sake of peace.

'I don't think you should do this,' Alexei told her bluntly before she got into the SUV to head back to the airport. I should come with you.'

The thought of Alexei standing by listening, while Lauren brandished her unashamedly rapacious take on how to live life and make a profit, only made Billie cringe. 'No, of course you shouldn't. I'll fly back here tomorrow,' she promised abruptly and watched the sardonic tightening of his handsome mouth ease into a more relaxed line.

In the limo that wafted her through the London streets that evening towards the hotel where her mother was staying, Billie was rigid with tension. Clearly feeling flush after the money she had earned from selling the story to the newspaper, her mother was staying in a plush suite. When she opened the door to Billie, her tangled blonde hair and the skimpy purple dress she wore, not to mention her unsteady gait, made it clear that she had been drinking heavily.

'Even when we were kids, Hilary could never wait to tell tales on me,' Lauren complained sulkily. 'I suppose you're here to read the Riot Act.'

'No, it's a little more basic than that. All my life I tried not to be too much of a burden to you and since I started earning, I've always been generous with money as well,' Billie said quietly. 'So why is it that the minute you get the chance, you stick a knife in my back?'

Lauren pulled a face. 'You're such a goody-goody, Billie. There's nothing of me in you, not in your looks, not in your nature either. How could you ever understand what it feels like to be me? I've had a lousy life because I had you when I was too young to know any better. Most men don't want a woman with another man's kid.'

'I don't recall that holding you back much,' Billie responded drily, refusing to listen to the self-pitying emotional blackmail that had been coming her way since she was very young. 'You had loads of boyfriends when I was a child but you never seemed to want to hang onto one in those days because I think you always thought there might be someone better round the next corner.'

'That was a damned sight healthier than falling drearily in love with my boss and spending years pining for him while living like a vestal virgin!' Lauren sneered at her daughter.

'Is that a little taste of what you've put in this newspaper article?' Billie demanded fiercely.

'Wouldn't you like to know?' Lauren taunted, throwing her daughter a smug look of superiority. 'But you'll have to wait a few weeks to read it like everybody else.'

'A few weeks...why a few weeks?' Billie questioned.

Her mother shrugged. 'How should I know? Maybe they wanted to check all the details out first.'

'You don't even care that it was my privacy

which you sold, do you? But to make use of photos of *Nicky*…'

Lauren laughed out loud at that rebuke. 'He's a gorgeous baby—you should be proud of him. Anyway, why are you here fussing? Haven't you got what you always wanted? So why be so mean when it comes to me? After all, you've got Alexei Drakos and that ring on your finger and pots and pots of money.'

'I've also got a mother who embarrasses the hell out of me,' Billie admitted painfully. 'How could you do this to us? You know how much value Alexei sets on privacy. You know our marriage is…rocky right now. I'm ashamed that you would sell our secrets and not even care how much distress you cause.'

Her mother was too busy topping up her glass of wine to pay much heed to that reproach. She gulped down a couple of mouthfuls and then glared at her daughter, who was watching her. Lauren spluttered angrily, *'What?'*

Billie realised that the older woman didn't care about what she'd said or about what she had done. She wasn't feeling guilty and she wasn't apologising either. Billie lifted her chin, determined not to show weakness or the engrained forgiving spirit that she had always employed with her feckless parent. 'I don't want anything more to do with you,' she declared sickly.

'Is that Alexei's order? I wondered how long it would be before he made you cut me out of your life,' Lauren framed, drunkenly gesticulating with her glass so that drops of wine spattered the pale carpet. 'But I don't care…I don't need any of you. All you've ever done is hold me back like deadweight. I want to be free. I want to do as I like without someone always raining on my parade.'

'Fine.' Billie walked to the door, shaken and deeply hurt by the older woman's complete lack of emotion. She loved her mother; she always had. Looking out for Lauren had been a need and a duty etched on her soul even as a child, yet with hindsight she finally had to acknowledge that her mother had never shown her affection and had more often made her feel like a burden whose very existence had prevented Lauren from enjoying the freedom she craved.

In a daze Billie got into the lift and travelled down to the hotel foyer. It was a moment before she recognised Helios, ostensibly browsing tourist brochures at the concierge's desk, but she was quick to recognise the movement of his head, which sent her away from the front exit towards a side entrance. A limousine, different from the one she had arrived in, was by the kerb. Only as Helios swept open the door for her did she see that Alexei was in the vehicle waiting for her.

'What on earth are you doing here?' she gasped in complete surprise, running her attention over him to note that he was still wearing the same suit he had worn earlier and, what was more, in defiance of his usual perfect grooming, was badly in need of a shave. 'And how did you get here so quickly?'

'It was a last-minute decision. I came by helicopter—I flew myself,' he advanced, searching her wan, tight face with an intensity that was unwelcome to her in her fragile emotional state. 'How was Lauren?'

'A-awful.' Billie stammered out that one word and feared that the tears would fall if she tried to say more. 'Drunk,' she finally added a minute later in grudging explanation.

Alexei skimmed a reflective knuckle down over the trail of a tear stain on her cheekbone. 'And she's a nasty drunk, isn't she?'

Billie gulped and nodded jerkily, and as she quivered like a tuning fork set on high vibration Alexei closed a comforting arm round her slim body to pull her close. Her eyes overflowed and she buried her wet face in his shoulder, drinking in the wonderfully welcome familiar smell of him, composed of an exclusive designer fragrance, essential masculinity and a unique hint of a scent that was simply him. She wanted to cling and sob but she wouldn't let herself drop her defences to that extent. Yet it meant so much to her that he had made himself available, had somehow understood how traumatic it would be for her to confront her mother. 'She wasn't even sorry!' she gasped strickenly.

'She needs rehab,' Alexei told her afresh. 'But that decision has to come from her to do any good.'

Billie snorted disbelief of that ever happening, although she was beginning to come round to his conviction that her mother did have a serious problem with alcohol. 'Where's Nicky?'

'Still in France. I thought it would be cruel to trail him back to London for the sake of one night,' Alexei confessed above her head, the dark, sexy timbre of his deep drawl quivering down her taut spinal column. 'Have you eaten yet?'

'I'm too tired to feel hungry.'

As she tripped up clumsily over her own feet in the smart hallway of the town house Alexei bent down and scooped her up into his arms. 'You're shattered,' he censured and paused only to speak to the housekeeper about dinner before carrying Billie upstairs.

It was quite a while since she had had cause

to go upstairs in the town house. For the long months of his engagement she had regarded the upper floor as Calisto's territory and she still felt that way now when Alexei took her into the magnificent master bedroom. When she gazed at the big bed, opulently draped in rich purple and olive shades chosen by the Greek woman, she could imagine all too well how good Calisto's blonde mane of hair, sparkling white smile and long leggy limbs would have looked against such a backdrop.

'I've ordered some food for you. After you've eaten get some sleep,' Alexei urged, settling her down on the bed and flipping off her shoes for her.

He settled down on the edge of the bed. A meal arrived on a tray and she discovered that she was hungrier than she had realised. 'You don't need to stay with me,' she told him.

Keen dark golden eyes rested on her. 'You're still upset…'

'I'm dreading what Lauren might have told

the newspaper,' Billie parried with a rueful grimace.

'Sticks and stones,' Alexei quipped lazily. 'Don't read it. Nothing that's printed should have the slightest impact on us.'

At that assurance, Billie shot him a wry glance. 'That wasn't your attitude when you saw that photo of Damon and me on the beach.'

Alexei's big powerful frame tensed. His strong jaw line clenched, his brilliant gaze veiling. 'That was different.'

'How?'

'Damon Marios has always had the hots for you.'

'That's nonsense. For goodness' sake, he married Ilona.'

'Only because he blew his chances with you as a teenager. You were his first love and he was yours. For a lot of people that creates a bond that's hard to shake off.'

'I could never see him the same way after that day he pretended not to be with me on the ferry,' Billie confided. 'I was always the outsider on the island, but he made me feel like dirt when he ignored me that day.'

Alexei curved an arm round her slight shoulders. 'He was an idiot. I was pleasantly surprised when you didn't forgive him for it.'

'I didn't like what you said about him that day but it was true and that's why you should know that I would never get involved again with Damon.'

Alexei compressed his wide sensual mouth. 'I just don't like him around you. You're my wife now. He should respect that. He shouldn't be so familiar with you. An honourable man respects those boundaries. You're a woman, you don't understand.'

Setting aside the tray because she was full, Billie released a drowsy laugh of disagreement. 'Oh, I understand you perfectly. You'd like a tag on my ankle engraved with your name.'

'This is serious. It's got nothing to do with possessiveness or jealousy,' Alexei hastened to declare in a tone of authority. 'It's simply a question of what's right.'

'I know. I can be serious too. I don't like this bed because Calisto picked the bedding and once slept here with you,' Billie confided chattily. 'But I'm not expecting you to drag the bed out and burn it for my benefit. It's simply a question of what's reasonable.'

Perplexed by that unexpected turning of the tables and that particular comparison, Alexei turned his stunning dark golden eyes on her. 'I'll have all the beds changed.'

'But that would be unreasonable and extravagant,' Billie pointed out gently to underline her point. 'Some things we just have to live with.'

Alexei sprang off the bed and looked down at her with brooding dark-as-night eyes. 'I'm not living with you holding hands with Damon Marios. The next time I find him with a hand anywhere near you I'll *kill* him!' he intoned in a raw undertone. 'And I don't care if that's unreasonable.'

With a sleepy sigh as the door snapped shut on Alexei's hot-headed exit, Billie rested her head back on the pillows and contemplated the reality that she was married to a guy who was infinitely more possessive of her and her affections than she had ever properly appreciated. Her friendship with Damon was perfectly innocent but, clearly, it really did get under Alexei's skin. Lying there thinking about it, she realised that even when she had worked for him Alexei had always acted as though he had a prior claim to her and a right to interfere in her private life. She should never have allowed him to behave that way, but until that moment she had never quite seen the extent of his possessiveness.

Now it brought a pained smile to her lips to recall the number of women she had watched swan through his life to pass through his various beds round the world. She had writhed with jealousy and envy and had cried herself asleep more than once over Alexei's volatile love life, but nobody had caused her to shed more tears than Calisto Bethune, who she had once believed had his heart as well as his body. But at that point Billie took a pause for more considered reflection. She was beginning to recognise that, now that she was Alexei's wife, it was time for her to exercise more sense and control her jealousy and her suspicions.

To be fair, Alexei had followed her to London purely to be there for her when she emerged in distress from her meeting with her recalcitrant mother. She was astonished that he had made such an effort on her behalf, and that he had understood her strained relationship with Lauren well enough to grasp that she would be upset and in need of support. But there had been other occasions in her long acquaintance with Alexei when he had shown himself to be equally thoughtful, she reminded herself ruefully. When had she chosen to forget that? That Alexei, without any prompting from her, had shown up to offer her that support and sympathy meant a great deal to Billie, particularly when sixth sense warned her that he had no time for Lauren at all and even less patience with her shenanigans.

Billie dozed off for several hours and wakened after midnight to find that she was still wearing her clothes. Suppressing a sigh, she got up, stripped off and dragged a nightdress out of her case before taking a shower to freshen up. Through the communicating door with the adjoining bedroom, she could hear distant strains of the television news playing and realised that that must be where Alexei was sleeping. Of course, after she had refused him that night at Hazlehurst, she mused wryly, he was unlikely to share the same room with her. After drying off her damp hair, she got back into bed and doused the lights. For half an hour she tossed and turned, thinking about Alexei, wishing he were with her, missing him, feeling deprived. And then suddenly she sat up, asked herself if she was a woman or a mouse, and got out of bed again.

She didn't knock on the communicating door and when she opened it the room was in darkness. 'It's only me,' she announced, feeling horrendously self-conscious.

'I didn't think it was a burglar,' Alexei murmured huskily.

In the faint light seeping round the edges of the

blinds, she picked out the dim shape of the bed and headed for it like a homing pigeon. Pushing back the duvet, she slid beneath it and wriggled across the cool expanse of the mattress until she found the hot, hard heat of him.

'You do realise that there will be consequences if you stay, *yineka mou*?' Alexei prompted thickly, one lean hand splaying across the feminine swell of her hip to press her into suggestive contact with the insistent swell of his growing erection.

Dry-mouthed and breathless, Billie snuggled into him, her heart pounding like an overwound clock. 'I was hoping so,' she admitted with a wanton little squirm of her hips in encouragement. 'I mean, I am returning to France with you tomorrow.'

Alexei rolled her under his lean powerful body and kissed her breathless. He tasted of wine and sex and the urgency pulsing through him lit her up like a blazing fire inside. 'So that we can enjoy the honeymoon we never had,' he breathed in a voice full of erotic promise.

'That's not the only r-reason I'm coming to France,' she stammered as he carried her fingers down to his hard male heat and the need in her leapt like a flame fanned into a blaze by the wind. She quivered, plunged her other hand impatiently into his luxuriant black hair and dragged his mouth back down onto hers. Her excitement licking out of her control, she trembled with hungry longing and it was long past dawn before she finally slept again.

CHAPTER TEN

OVER four weeks later, Billie awakened in the glorious illuminating light that Provence was famous for and didn't waste any time in checking the other side of the big bed, because she knew she would be alone. A lie-in for Alexei was staying in bed past dawn and it was now after ten. Stifling a drowsy yawn, she stretched with voluptuous pleasure, a smug smile tilting her mouth when the movement made her aware of all the little aches and pains of a woman enjoying an active and adventurous love life.

In that department, Alexei was incomparable, she reflected with helpless satisfaction. It also seemed to her as though every time they made love she felt closer to him. Did he still think of their intimacy as just sex? She didn't know, hadn't asked, and had no plans to enquire or pick holes in the happiness she had found with him. What did the words matter anyway? What really mattered was how Alexei behaved and the connection between them was very strong. With Nicky thrown into the mix and fully shared, that bond had definitely deepened.

It had been a relief that, as yet, no tell-all revelations had appeared in print following Lauren's interviews with a journalist. But the threat of what her mother might have said still hung over Billie's head and bothered her in uneasy moments. After all, intelligence warned her that no newspaper would have paid Lauren a lot of money for information that they had no intention of publishing. She hadn't heard a word from the older woman, who was still in London living it up on the proceeds of her betrayal, according to Hilary.

As Billie laid out clothes after a quick shower she marvelled that she and Alexei had been staying at their rambling comfortable chateau for almost five weeks. Their days had slowly fallen into a pattern: mornings, Alexei usually worked and often she worked with him. Alexei had, on average, only left the South of France once a week for important meetings and was delegating all that he could.

Dressed in a blue sundress, Billie walked out onto the stone balcony to survey the timeless landscape of vineyards, lavender fields and distant cliffs. The views still enchanted her. Sometimes she and Alexei walked down the cobble-stoned street to have coffee and a croissant in the village square. Occasionally they dined at the quaint little restaurant built into the fortified walls that surrounded the village. And what she loved most about the area was that, aside of the attention Nicky attracted as he smiled out of his buggy, nobody took the slightest bit of notice of them. By common consent they had stayed away from the Côte D'Azur and the exclusive resorts where Alexei would be instantly recognisable and constantly approached.

An exquisite ruby-and-diamond ring in the design of a flower shone on Billie's finger in the glorious sunlight. Alexei had given it to her on the memorable night they went clubbing in a funky old warehouse in Marseille and he'd taught her to dance the salsa.

'What's that for?' she had asked when he gave her the ring.

And Alexei had laughed. 'You're not supposed to say that. It makes a gift sound like some sort of payment and although I have given many gifts in that line in the past you don't come into that category. Of course I could tell you it's because you're great in bed, or because you're beautiful, or because you're the only lover I've ever had with hair the colour of a sunset.' At that point in his teasing little speech, Alexei had suddenly frowned and his gaze had taken on a curious abstracted quality. 'I saw the true attraction of your hair the first time I saw it in sunlight…and I told you,' he had completed with sudden harsh emphasis as he frowned. 'I told you that on the night after the funeral.'

'You've finally remembered something!' Billie had exclaimed with pleasure. 'Do you remember how you felt that night? What you were thinking about?'

Alexei had tensed. 'Oh, yes,' he had confirmed, but he had not gone on to share any revelations on that score, although it had seemed to her that he was rather distant for the rest of that day and, indeed, the days that followed. Her elation that he had at last recalled some facet of that evening had gradually dwindled when he'd failed to mention it again.

Sometimes they played at being tourists, going further afield to sleepy hilltop villages where they wandered round market stalls piled high with fresh produce in dazzling colours and bought home-made bread, olives, honey and also armfuls of lavender that Billie loved to use to scent the chateau. To Alexei's amusement, Marie, their housekeeper, never failed to point out that produce just as good, indeed most probably superior, could be bought right on the doorstep.

Billie had learned a lot more than she had thought she needed to know about the running of an organic vineyard. Alexei took a knowledgeable interest in every step of the process and was currently teaching her to differentiate between an acceptable wine and a superlative one. Only the previous year the Domaine Claudel label had won an award and Alexei was eager to build on that success. Billie was less interested in the wine than she was in Alexei's enthusiasm in the face of a challenge.

Now she descended the stairs and frowned when she heard Nicky howling. She followed the source of his cries to the library where Alexei had abandoned his attempt to work to pull his son out of the wastepaper basket he had knocked over.

Having learned to crawl early, Nicky had rapidly become a little menace. Suddenly he couldn't be depended on to stay where he was put any more and if there was anything dangerous within reach he seemed to home in on it. He had trailed out the contents of drawers and cupboards, shredded books and burrowed into pot plants. He was a baby on a demolition mission, set on causing the maximum possible destruction to his surroundings.

'No, you can't do that,' Alexei was telling his son as he lifted him, and as the little boy snatched a pen off the desk added. 'No, you can't have that either.'

From the doorway, Billie watched as Nicky breathed in deep and bawled in bad temper, his lower lip jutting with baby-rage at the restrictions being put on his freedom.

'And that's not going to get you anywhere either,' Alexei asserted, dropping down to lift one of the toys on the floor and hand it to his enraged son.

Nicky flung the toy away and howled even louder.

Alexei sat down and let his son claw his way upright by holding onto his jacket. Nicky jumped and his temper cleared like magic, for there was nothing he liked more at present than the ability to stand upright and bounce with energetic thoroughness.

Arms wrapping round Nicky to support him

in a hug, Alexei cast languorous dark golden eyes across the room to Billie's slender blue-clad figure and he smiled his heartbreakingly beautiful smile. 'I thought you were never going to surface today.'

'And whose fault is it that I'm so tired?' Billie fired back readily before she could think better of that comment.

Alexei raised a sleek ebony brow in surprise at that question. 'I distinctly remember being woken up in the early hours by a very demanding woman.'

Billie turned hot pink at the memory. Sometimes she just stretched out and found him in the bed and desire would roar through her like an express train. She just couldn't quite believe that Alexei was now hers to touch and love. Proximity to him had made her greedy and sexier than she had ever thought she could be. The knowledge that he always seemed to want her had lifted her confidence. She wore lingerie that would have made her blush just months earlier; occasionally, she wore very little at all.

Nicky rested his little dark head down on Alexei's shoulder and sagged, long lashes sweeping on his cheekbones.

'I'll put him down for a nap,' Billie said.

Alexei slid lithely upright and led the way up the staircase. Billie changed her son and made him comfortable in his cot in the room next to their own. Kasma was out for the day and, although a local girl took over in her absence to ensure that the young Greek woman didn't have to work too many hours on the trot, Alexei and Billie regularly took charge of their son and saw to his needs without help.

Alexei stared down into the cot where Nicky was half-heartedly trying to reach for his little pink toes and then he glanced across at Billie. 'I'd like another child.'

Astonished by that abrupt confession and unprepared for it, Billie frowned.

'I wasn't part of it when you were carrying Nikolos. I missed out on everything,' Alexei pointed out levelly.

'You know why I didn't tell you,' Billie reminded him defensively.

'I know you decided that my girlfriend was more important to me than my unborn child,' Alexei countered. 'But that was *your* mistake. I would have put my child's needs first, just as my father once did. It's a shame that you didn't give me the chance to prove that to you firsthand.'

A frisson of fierce annoyance washed away all the warm feelings that Billie had experienced watching Alexei handle their son with such patience, common sense and warmth. But his skill as a parent aside, wasn't she entitled to have some pride? To want a man who was not simply *with* her because she had fallen accidentally pregnant? With hindsight, Billie now recognised that it was the fear of Alexei feeling responsible for her because she was pregnant rather than freely choosing to be with her that had made her stay silent after she had conceived. Calisto had been more competition than Billie had felt up to taking on and challenging. She needed to be wanted for herself, not for her son's benefit. But just how deep did that attitude of Alexei's go? Was he only set on showing her what a wonderful guy he could be in retrospect? Or was their honeymoon ninety per cent fake as he made a very clever and rational attempt to give their marriage sound and lasting foundations? That suspicion sent a shiver down her sensitive spine.

'I think one child is enough for us right now,' she responded quietly.

Stunning golden eyes as bright as sunlight raked over her tense, uneasy expression. 'You still don't trust me. Do you think I'm so selfish that I would suggest having another child *without* the intention of our marriage lasting?'

'It's not a matter of trust,' Billie reasoned hurriedly. 'I just need more time with you to believe that.'

'Nicky has roused emotions in me that I never realised I could feel,' Alexei volunteered, startling her with that admission. 'You're surprised... I'm surprised. But I was bored with my life as it was. I'm much more ready to be a family man than I ever appreciated, *yineka mou.*'

'That's great,' Billie told him, but she was not convinced enough to risk a second pregnancy on the strength of that declaration. When she lost her figure, he might not find her as attractive, she reasoned uncomfortably. He was and always would be a male to whom a high-voltage sex life meant a great deal and pregnancy would definitely make a difference to their relationship. That was not a chance she wanted to take.

'You saw far too much of my life as a playboy,' Alexei groaned, folding her slim, curvy body into his arms. 'That's where the problem lies.'

'I'm not prejudiced—'

'How can you lie to me like that?' Alexei censured. 'You disapproved of my sex life from the day you met me.'

'I'm not lying,' she said uncomfortably.

'You never could hide how you felt either,' Alexei continued with sardonic cool. 'You'd get a stony look on your face and go all stiff and prissy, and your voice would go cold.'

Billie was thoroughly disconcerted by that recital of her reactions.

Unexpectedly, Alexei's lean bronzed features broke into an unholy grin of amusement as he pulled her closer. 'You really were a jealous little cat from the word go!'

'That's not true,' Billie mumbled, refusing to meet his shrewd gaze, as she had not once mentioned love since her return to France, had wrenched the very word from her thoughts and buried it deep. In Alexei's radius she could only feel that the less said about love and all such sentiments, the better.

'And there I was leading a perfectly normal life as a single man,' Alexei lamented.

'You were...*wild*,' Billie rebutted without an instant of hesitation.

'But in some dark little corner of your head, you *love* wild,' Alexei murmured huskily, shifting against her in a lithe movement to acquaint her with the hard male heat at his groin.

Loving him as much as she thrilled to that wildness, Billie trembled, feeling the surge of heat and moisture between her legs, wishing she had more control over her responses. He pressed her slender length to him and bent his head to kiss her with a raw, urgent hunger that left her struggling to breathe. He had made love to her for half of the night but now he wanted her again and she rejoiced in that knowledge, which made her feel secure and needed. She let him back her into their bedroom on legs that felt as weak as cotton-wool supports. But she was no passive partner, for she dragged his jacket off him and embarked on his shirt buttons while exchanging passionate kisses that made her heartbeat race.

'I think you should just stay in bed all day,' Alexei confided, letting his teeth graze a particularly tender place on her neck and suppressing a groan as she wriggled against his long powerful thighs. 'Getting dressed is hardly worth your while. I can't get enough of you, *yineka mou*.'

He was pulling down the straps on her shoulders, accessing the scented hollow between her breasts and the pale upper slopes before he found the zip and the dress fell to her waist. He dealt with the light bra that merely uplifted the ripe swell of her flesh and he caught a straining pink nipple in his mouth to ravish it, even as he pushed up her skirt, ripped her delicate chiffon panties out of his path and found the sweet damp warmth of her silken flesh. A moment later, he braced her back against the wall, hoisted her against him and brought her down on him. She cried out in shivering excitement as he sank deep into her slick wet heat and after only a few strokes he moved her, tumbling her down on the bed and plunging into her tight depths over and over again with an erotic dominance that excited her beyond belief. She hit a shattering high of pleasure and she arched up to him and cried out at the convulsive strength of the climax gripping her. Dizzy satisfaction engulfed her as Alexei reached the same peak and shuddered in her arms.

'Did I hurt you? Was I too rough?' Alexei queried, breathing heavily.

'I'm fine…better than fine…on another planet,' she mumbled, struggling to find the right words to encompass her wonderful sense of well-being.

Alexei gave her a wicked smile that tilted her heart on its axis and crushed her close to his bare chest. 'It just gets better and better with you,' he sighed, dropping a kiss on her parted lips. 'You're an amazing find, *moraki mou.*'

A slew of phone calls disrupted dinner that evening. When Billie asked if there was a crisis of some kind Alexei fended off her questions with a shuttered look on his lean dark features. Bemused by his behaviour, she went to bed alone. In the morning she wakened to the sound of a text reaching her mobile phone and, before she reached for it, noticed to her surprise that the pillow beside hers was untouched. The message was from Hilary. It informed her that Lauren's story had appeared that morning and Hilary had faxed a copy of the piece to the chateau. It also urged Billie not to pay heed to what her aunt termed 'spiteful drivel', but Billie's apprehension about the unsavoury nature of her mother's revelations rose to new heights.

A knock on the bedroom door heralded the arrival of a breakfast tray that could only have been ordered for her by Alexei. Striving to remain calm but, for once, impervious to the stunning view, Billie sat out at a table on the wrought-iron girded balcony and ate fresh fruit. She shredded her croissant and then lost interest in eating it while she wondered what tales her mother might have shared with the press. Who would dare to disbelieve stories told by her own flesh and blood? And the answer to that was: anyone who had ever enjoyed a personal acquaintance with Lauren, who was always willing to stretch the boundaries of the truth to make a good story.

The sound of the bedroom door snapping shut made her turn her head. Alexei strolled out onto the stone balcony, a lean powerful figure sheathed in close-fitting beige chino pants and a black T-shirt. Luxuriant black hair glinting in the sunlight, stunning golden eyes semi-screened by spiky dark lashes, he looked jaw-droppingly beautiful to her attentive gaze. Her heart seemed to jump behind her breastbone and her mouth ran dry, but neither appreciative response prevented her from noting that he was pale and tense with just the suggestion of gritted teeth behind the set of his stubborn, passionate mouth.

'You've been reading Lauren's interview with the *Sunday Globe*,' Billie guessed in a hot-cheeked rush. While Hilary had assumed that their location abroad would make it difficult for them to gain easy access to that article, Billie knew that Alexei had the British newspapers flown in every day.

Alexei sent her a questioning glance.

'Hilary texted me and then faxed a copy here—'

'It came through but I chucked it in the bin,' Alexei admitted. 'It'll only upset you.'

'She's my mother. I have every intention of reading it.'

His brilliant eyes veiled as if he had been prepared for that response. 'Then you might as well know the worst now. Lauren has accused me of having an affair with Calisto...'

The numbness of shock possessed Billie's lower limbs and the colour bled from her cheeks. For several deeply unpleasant seconds she felt physically sick and in the act of rising from the chair she dropped down again and gripped the arms with clenched fingers. 'That may be my fault,' she muttered with a sudden groan. 'Before the DNA results arrived and I saw you at Hazlehurst, I saw a photo of you with Calisto in Paris and I have to admit that I *was* suspicious…'

'If I had still wanted Calisto, I would never have dumped her in the first place or moved on to marry you,' Alexei spelt out, his arrogant head held high, his jaw line at an uncompromising angle. 'You have to learn to trust me, Billie. There will always be allegations of that nature made against me. Like my father, I'll often be a target and I won't have that kind of nonsense causing trouble between us. I've already called in my lawyers. I intend to sue on this occasion.'

It was at that point that Billie realised that Alexei had sought her out quite deliberately to tell her what was in that article before she could read it. A pre-emptive strike and very much in the bold, buccaneering Drakos style, she reflected painfully. How did she trust a male so clever and manipulative that he even knew how best to sidestep claims of infidelity?

Billie pushed away her plate and got up. Alexei was regarding her with expectancy. Was he expecting an apologetic hug and the assurance that of course she believed him? It hurt that her mother could have plunged them into such a confrontation, but at the back of her mind she couldn't help thinking that had Alexei been willing to be more frank with her she would never have cherished such qualms about Calisto.

'I'll get dressed,' she said without any expression at all.

'If you go outside, stay away from the front gates—a bunch of paps are conducting a stake-out.'

'Oh…' Biting her lip, Billie looked away, finally registering that Lauren had clearly managed to create quite a splash with her revelations. Her mother, she thought sadly, would be revelling in the limelight. She only hoped that the story Lauren had already sold would be the one and only time she talked about her daughter's marriage in public. And that when the dust finally settled there would still *be* a marriage to conserve, she thought painfully.

When she finally held the relevant newspaper in her hand, she felt as if a cold hand were trailing down her spine. 'I don't need you hovering!' she told Alexei, who was poised by a tall window with Nicky clasped in his arms. 'Certainly not with Nicky in tow. I don't want him to hear us arguing.'

Level dark golden eyes held hers with fierce determination. 'Then don't read it…'

And so intense were his look and tone that she almost succumbed, until common sense warned her that she would not be able to live with her ignorance. The fine bones of her face taut below her skin, she shook her head in urgent dismissal of that advice and walked out to the garden in search of the privacy in which to read. The hot golden light of noon drained the borders in the walled garden of their vibrant colour and the blessed shade below the oak tree beckoned like a long cold drink in scorching temperatures.

The whole focus of the newspaper article was encapsulated by a devastating photograph of Alexei kissing Calisto in a Parisian street. In total shock at the sight of their two bodies plastered together and so close, Billie flinched and speed-read through the claim that Alexei had plunged back into an affair with Calisto within days of walking out on his bride the previous month. So, it *was* true, she reflected sickly. There were Calisto and Alexei captured together in black and white, the ultimate proof of infidelity, which even Alexei could not dispute. Evidently all her worst fears had been right on target.

Her heart thudding sickly inside her, she skimmed over the pictures of their son and read on. Surprisingly, Lauren had not overly embroidered the tale of how Billie had come to fall in love with Alexei while she worked for him. She'd described how the stressful hours of Billie's busy working days had been punctuated with the constant procession of gorgeous women with whom

Alexei had amused himself and Billie's growing heartbreak while she'd watched. Lauren had had a thoroughly cynical take on Alexei's behaviour and had accused him of having 'used' her lovesick daughter for comfort in the wake of his parents' deaths and then cruelly ditching her when Calisto had reappeared, divorced and available again. Lauren had also implied that he must have known Billie had fallen pregnant and had sent her off on a supposed career break to deliberately conceal the fact.

A slight noise made Billie's head fly up, green eyes wide and pained when she saw Alexei standing on the gravel path staring at her with a curiously raw expression in his dark eyes.

'That photo of me kissing Calisto is almost two years old,' he breathed harshly. 'There *is* no affair.'

Unwilling to even listen, Billie turned her bright head away. Whichever way she looked at the problem, Alexei had betrayed her with the other woman, because in forgetting their intimacy after the funeral he had been unfaithful.

Was it unjust of her to feel that way when he had given her no promise of commitment or exclusivity that night?

'Billie…that is an *old* photo, taken long before our marriage,' Alexei repeated determinedly.

'How do I believe that? I mean, I know Calisto was more than willing to renew your relationship, regardless of the fact that you had married me,' she argued helplessly. 'She was even grateful I had given you a son because she didn't want to run the risk of spoiling her figure with a pregnancy—'

Alexei was frowning, ebony brows pleated. 'When did she tell you that?'

'When I saw her in Paris. She said you wouldn't leave me with custody of Nicky, that you would take him off me and that she was willing to help you bring him up!'

Alexei stared at her in frank disbelief. 'Why didn't you tell me that before? How could you listen to such ridiculous lies?' he demanded accusingly. 'I *know* how much you and my son mean to each other. No matter what happens between us, I would never part you from him—'

'You parted us a month ago,' Billie reminded him.

'For a matter of hours, and only to get you here in order to give our marriage a fighting chance!' Alexei protested in heated disagreement. 'You're a wonderful mother and our son will always need you. How could you have listened to Calisto's poisonous claims?'

'How could you put her in your house in Paris and expect me to accept it?'

His dark gaze gleaming golden, Alexei flung up lean brown hands in a furious show of frustration. 'Because I *owed* her! I was the one who changed my mind about our relationship. She didn't change, I did. In the name of God, Billie, how could you not have told me about what happened between us after the funeral? Didn't it occur to you that I might have forgotten but that I might feel that I had *lost* something, even if I didn't know what that something was?'

Wide-eyed and shaken by that counter charge,

Billie watched him stride closer. 'Lost something?' she repeated uncertainly. 'I'm not sure I know what you mean—'

'We forged a connection that night deep enough to haunt me when I lost it again,' Alexei argued. 'But I had to remember how I felt that night to realise why I'd ended up charging into a rebound affair with Calisto.'

'You're saying you remember being with me that night now?' Billie questioned weakly. 'If that's true, why didn't you tell me?'

Alexei released a shaken laugh that carried more bitterness than amusement. 'Why did it never occur to you that I would be ashamed of what I would remember of that night?'

Her brow indented. *Ashamed?* She almost bleated out the word again in dismay, but she was fed up of trying and failing to guess what he meant and this time she said nothing.

'Of course, I was ashamed,' Alexei grated in a low driven voice. 'I took advantage of you.'

Tenderness touched her frantic thoughts, slow-ing the flow of them. 'No, you didn't. You were lonely, shaken up, vulnerable...'

'And I took advantage of you just like your mother has accused me of doing,' Alexei completed resolutely. 'But on the same night while I was with you I realised that I was very probably in love with you and that I had been for some time.'

Blinking rapidly, Billie gazed back at him with frowning force. 'But that's not possible!'

'You got under my skin...you infiltrated me and I didn't even know it was happening to me,' Alexei bit out with annoyance at his lack of self-knowledge on that score. 'Suddenly I was always comparing other women to you and you were winning hands down in every comparison—sex was just the next natural step that night but that shouldn't have been how it happened between us.'

'You weren't in love with me,' Billie told him flatly. 'And how else should we have become intimate? One doesn't always plan these things.'

'You deserved more from me than what you

got that night when I was drunk and confused and more than a little spooked by the weird way I was feeling,' Alexei extended wryly. 'When I was willing to wait until we were married—that respect and patience was a better demonstration of how I should have treated you from the first, *agapi mou*.'

My love, he'd called her, and Billie could hardly get her head around the staggering declaration engrained in that endearment. Her attention locked to his lean darkly handsome features, she breathed uncertainly. 'I just don't believe what I'm hearing from you!'

'When I fell down the steps and hit my head outside the guest suite, I forgot more than what we shared in your bed that night,' Alexei continued vehemently. 'I forgot how happy I was, how convinced I'd become that I had finally found the right woman for me. Why the hell do you think that I took the risk of making love to you without contraception? That was so out of character for me, it should have screamed at you and convinced you that I was planning a lot more than a brief sexual encounter with you!'

And there was so much truth in that contention that Billie finally allowed herself to listen. In truth, she had noticed that he was not quite himself that night and some of the stuff he had said to her had seemed to indicate a greater degree of involvement with her than she might have expected. But she had been quick to dismiss any such hopes, even quicker to assume the worst of a male who had apparently so often treated sex like a takeaway meal—cheap and disposable and forgettable. Her own cynicism and low expectations, she recognised ruefully, had combined to ensure that she was reluctant to confront him with the facts of their intimacy. In the expectation of disillusionment, she had ironically ensured that disillusionment was exactly what she had received.

'I just assumed it would mean nothing to you and that maybe you forgot because you didn't *want* to remember it.'

Alexei compressed his lips. 'There may be

some truth in that angle, but not on the score of what happened between us. A few weeks ago, I did consult a psychiatrist about those hours I couldn't remember and he suggested that my mind could be reluctant to recall my grief for my parents that night. He was of the opinion, however, that since I had already contrived to recall one moment of those missing hours, I would eventually remember more. I did consider having hypnotherapy...'

'I had no idea you were that bothered about not having those memories,' Billie confided.

'Of course I was bothered. That encounter was central to our marriage and your attitude of distrust. I had to remember what I did that night to understand how horrific the experience must have been for you. One minute we were together and then the next, it was like it had never happened—'

'Yes, it was very painful,' Billie acknowledged unhappily, grateful he understood and astonished that he had seen a psychiatrist in an effort to deal with the issue and find a solution. 'But I really didn't know what to do about it. Staying quiet seemed the most sensible move on every count—of course I didn't think of what might happen if I fell pregnant. When did you remember it all?'

'I had a couple of small flashes and then, one morning, I woke up and the whole recollection was just there,' he revealed. 'I was shattered when I realised how I'd felt that night with you.'

'And you truly think you got involved with Calisto because you were on the rebound from me?' Billie whispered doubtfully.

'Didn't it ever cross your mind that Calisto and I had as much in common as a dog and a cat?' Alexei enquired drily. 'What drew me back to her was familiarity—my recollection of how I felt about her as a teenager and the fact I couldn't have her. Of course what I wanted then from a woman is not at all what I want now. It took me a while to appreciate that Calisto only married Bethune because at that time he was a better financial bet than I was, as a son still dependent on a father for support.'

Billie was afraid to have faith in what he was

telling her. It was true that he and Calisto had appeared to have nothing in common. She had wondered what he could see in a fashion model who shared none of his interests. But she had also known that love was reputedly blind and had feared that beauty and sex appeal had won out over common sense. Now when he told her otherwise she wanted so much to believe that message but she was afraid to.

'I thought you were so happy with her,' Billie framed.

'The first fine flush lasted…oh, all of five minutes,' Alexei confided, his handsome mouth forming a sardonic twist in acknowledgement. 'I refused to listen to my doubts because, as I told you, I was ready for something more, something deeper, and when Calisto reappeared it felt like fate.'

Billie winced. 'Fate can be cruel.'

Alexei frowned and nodded agreement. 'If only you had told me about us, at least I would have stopped and listened.'

'If you were infatuated with her, I don't know that you would have.'

'You didn't give me the chance,' he reminded her. 'In fact you assumed the worst of me at every stage and expected nothing. That was the real problem. That was what kept us apart.'

Billie reckoned that she had spent too long on the sidelines of Alexei's life watching him live up to his bad reputation to credit that he might behave differently with her. And yet, even as she recognised that fact, she also recognised that Alexei had always treated her with a lot more respect and kindness than he'd employed with the other women in his life. She had never been just an employee, forced to respect strict boundaries, and in the same way he had always looked out for her interests.

'Why did you really break up with Calisto?' Billie finally asked.

'She wasn't right for me. I don't want to do her down,' Alexei confessed ruefully, his strong jaw line hardening, 'but I saw her as she really was the day I found her screaming abuse at a toddler on *Sea Queen*.'

'On St George's Day, when you were entertaining the islanders on the yacht?' Billie questioned, referring to the saint's day when everyone who lived on Speros celebrated the holiday. 'What toddler?'

'The little boy you took to find his mother. Before that, he had bumped into Calisto and put chocolate handprints on her skirt. I found her shouting at him and the poor little chap was sobbing his heart out. I couldn't stay with a woman who could treat a young child like that, and when she turned her attention on you that same afternoon that was the last straw,' he admitted grimly. 'She has a vicious streak I can't accept.'

Well aware of how that vicious streak had offended and wounded other employees, Billie said nothing. Naturally she had known that Calisto had had character traits wholly at odds with Alexei's engrained sense of fairness and courtesy, but that Alexei could have found Calisto's verbal attack on her that same day intolerable touched her heart. Calisto had accused her of flirting with Alexei. Now all of a sudden Billie was appreciating that Alexei had cared even then about her, even if she hadn't realised it.

'I didn't love her,' Alexei breathed, reaching down to close his hands round Billie's and draw her upright. 'I never loved her. Why would I risk my marriage to sleep with her again?'

Her hands quivered in the warm hold of his and she lifted fearless eyes to him. 'You didn't care about our marriage when you walked out on me. You didn't believe that Nicky was your son either...'

His ebony brows drew together. 'Be fair. You took me by surprise and I was devastated by the fallout on our wedding night. You are the one woman in the world whom I've always totally trusted,' he reasoned urgently, and pink discomfiture coloured her upturned face with regret. 'And it did all sound crazy at the time.'

'You didn't love me when you married me...'

Long brown fingers framed her cheeks to hold her troubled eyes steady. 'I didn't *know* I loved you when I married you. I thought I was being so sensible choosing you when, all the time, you *were* the only choice. Because, right then, you were the only woman I wanted,' he told her ruefully. 'Then it all blew up in my face. I didn't know how I felt. I didn't even realise why it all hurt so much. I just felt betrayed.'

Her fingers stroked over his and gripped tight in apology. 'I know. I know how impossible I made it for you but there was no easy way to go about telling you.'

His lean hands held hers tight. 'Telling me the truth upfront,' he countered. 'Trusting me the same way I trust you—'

Sentenced to stillness by the tender look in his dark golden eyes, Billie breathed in deep. 'So, you're not chasing Calisto again?'

'No, and she's already called me to let me know that she has issued a public rebuttal to that effect,' Alexei incised and then, with an unexpected touch of amusement, 'Along with the news that she's got engaged again and she doesn't want rumours of an adulterous association with me to spoil that.'

'Engaged again? But to whom?' Billie prompted in astonishment.

'A very wealthy Parisian banker. He's a lot older than she is, but she says older men are more reliable and, since he already has adult children, he's not expecting her to have a child with him,' Alexei completed.

'But when I saw Calisto in Paris, she made it quite clear that she wanted you back.'

'But I didn't want her and the banker was obviously her back-up plan. I'm relieved she's found someone,' Alexei said wryly. 'I can hand over her affairs to an accountant with a clear conscience.'

And seeing his relief, Billie finally believed that only his sense of responsibility had urged him to go to Calisto's assistance after their relationship had ended. It was as if a weight fell off her shoulders and a dark shadow was jerked from her thoughts. With a sigh she leant forward and rested her head down on his shoulder. 'I'm relieved as well.'

'But you didn't need to be. I love you,' Alexei pointed out doggedly. 'The minute you started talking about divorcing me, I wised up fast. That was a really sensible move of yours—it brought me to my senses.'

'It wasn't a move!' Billie exclaimed in stark disconcertion at the charge. 'It seemed the only solution if you couldn't forgive me for keeping you in the dark about Nicky.'

Alexei bent his arrogant dark head and claimed her mouth with hot, hard brevity that left her breathless, her slim body curving into his and alight with the desire for more. 'The moment you threatened me with a divorce I got off my high horse. It brought me to my senses and I stopped wallowing in your sins. I didn't want to lose you, *agapi mou*,' he murmured, rubbing his knuckles down over her cheekbone in a tender gesture. 'I couldn't *bear* to lose you. I've spent the last few weeks trying to show you that but sometimes I feel like I'm banging my head up against a brick wall.'

'I was so jealous and insecure about Calisto that she came between me and my wits,' Billie confessed in a rush, finally allowing herself to believe that she was loved and revelling in the adoring intensity of his gaze on her face. 'You have been making me very happy, but I was so hurt when you didn't seem to feel anything when I told you how I felt about you.'

'I'm sorry. For a while I didn't think I could trust anything you said,' he confided candidly. 'I was angry, bitter and disappointed in you and it was a while before I could move on from that to concentrate on what's really important. And what's really important is that you *had* our son and now we have the rest of our lives to spend together.'

The rest of our lives. The warmth of his gaze, the buoyancy of his dark deep drawl wrapped round her vulnerable heart like a blanket of reassurance. She hugged him close, a pulse of happiness pounding through her as she let go of her fears and insecurities and finally felt free to claim her happy ending.

'I love you,' she whispered.

He drew her out of the shade of the oak tree into the bright sunlight and on into the dim cool of the chateau. But it was Billie who headed straight for the stairs and the privacy of their bedroom while throwing a half-embarrassed, half-teasing glance over her shoulder at him. Before they got there, however, another concern stole the lightness from her mood. 'We haven't even talked about Lauren, or what we're going to do about her,' she reminded him heavily.

Alexei swung her back to face him. 'We'll deal with her together,' he murmured with quiet resolve. 'She needs to respect our privacy as a family. But it's only thanks to that article that I know how long you've cared about me.'

Billie reddened and screened her eyes. 'I didn't want you to know that.'

'I cared about you too, *agapi mou*,' he traded softly. 'And in ways I couldn't count or explain. I never liked seeing you tired or cross or unwell. I always wanted to make you happy. I hated seeing you with another man. When I had no right to be, I was very possessive of you. Your friendship with Damon Marios really got to me and made me angry and jealous.'

'But it never was anything but a friendship.' Billie shivered as he ran down the zip on her dress and eased it down her arms, pausing to claim a hungry, driving kiss that went on and on and on because she was clinging to him with a heart that was pounding as hard as a road drill inside her chest.

'I love you like crazy,' she told him breathlessly as he tugged her down on the bed with him, finally accepting that he loved her and he was hers in every way that mattered. Suddenly she finally grasped why he had stealthily instructed that all the master-suite beds in his various homes were renewed. He was thinking about her feelings and doing what he could to acknowledge them.

'And you believe me about Calisto? I am suing the *Sunday Globe* over that photo of me with her,' Alexei breathed. 'I know now why Lauren's story wasn't published immediately—the paper was waiting and hoping to get proof that I was having an affair with Calisto, but when they couldn't they dug out an old photo instead.'

'I know you're not having an affair.' Billie gazed up at him with her heart in her eyes and his smile felt like sunshine on her skin. 'And if you're still in the mood, I have reconsidered: I would like to have another child soon.'

'That's a very sexy invitation, Mrs Drakos,' Alexei purred, disposing of his shirt with careless grace and baring a hair-roughened muscular torso that seemed to beg for the touch of her appreciative hands. 'Are you sure?'

'More sure than I've ever been about anything,' Billie confessed, regretting the hurt she knew she had inflicted when she was unable to give him her trust. There was love and tenderness in his expressive golden eyes and, although it felt as if it were the first time she was seeing those emotions, she knew they had been there in recent weeks as well, only she had been too blind to recognise them for what they were. She had been

equally thick-headed when it came to acknowledging that the average boss didn't treat his PA
to hot chocolate topped with melted marshmal-
lows at the end of a difficult day, or send her off
on a spa break. Nor, if he was Alexei Drakos,
did he offer to cut down on the other women for
a mere fancy. But she had not read those signs,
had thought too little of herself to recognise that
she was special to him.

'I'll never stop loving you,' he swore with
all the passion and intensity of his powerful
temperament.

'Well, I did try to get over you lots of times,
but it just never worked,' Billie admitted more
prosaically.

And Alexei laughed with considerable
appreciation…

Eighteen months later, Billie tucked her infant
daughter, Kolena, into her cot.

Dark-eyed and red-haired, Kolena was a de-
lightful mixture of her parents' genes. Nicky
hung over the side of the cot watching his sister

and pushed a stuffed toy at her hand. The little starfish fingers closed round the bear, but then the baby's eyes slid drowsily shut.

'Kolena's sleeping again,' Nicky complained, his little boy's restive body humming with suppressed energy.

'It's been a long day for her.' Billie smiled as she thought back on a day of great enjoyment at the christening party held at Hazlehurst Manor. For the first time in her life she had contrived to have both of her parents in the same room. It was true that at the outset of laying eyes on her former fiancée and daughter's father, Lauren had merely nodded frostily across the room at Desmond, but her resistance had crumpled when Desmond complimented her on her continuing youthful good looks. Billie had last seen her mother and father chatting companionably at the buffet and was relieved that her parents could now meet without any awkwardness.

Of course, the past eighteen months had proved more than usually eventful for her mother and had led to a much-changed lifestyle. Lauren had stayed on in London to paint the town red and, within six months of the publication of the story she had sold, she had spent all the money she had earned from it and the hotel where she'd been in residence had contacted Alexei, just before throwing Lauren out onto the street for unpaid bills. At that point, Hilary had persuaded her sister to go into rehab for, by that stage, there had been little doubt that Lauren had a problem with alcohol. But, unhappily, the treatment hadn't worked on that occasion, probably because Lauren had merely surrendered to Hilary's arguments rather than acting on a genuine need to seek help for herself. It had been Billie who'd taken charge of her mother the next time that her lifestyle had got her into trouble—because, by then, Hilary had been abroad on her honeymoon. Now Lauren herself was willing to acknowledge that she had a serious addiction problem.

This second stay in rehab, followed by regular attendance at AA meetings, had helped Lauren to stay off the booze and she and her daughter were getting on much better since then. Sobriety had softened Lauren's sharp tongue and lessened her dramas, while happiness had made Billie more accepting of her mother's weaknesses.

The previous year, Hilary had married Stuart McGregor, the captain of Alexei's yacht, in a quiet ceremony. Still working on her history book, which had since found a publisher, Hilary was—to her astonishment and delight—now four months pregnant with her first child. Up until then the little terrier, Skye, which Alexei had given to Billie on their wedding day, had been the apple of her aunt's eye. Skye had, after all, lived with Hilary while Billie and Alexei were enjoying their extended honeymoon in France, and by the time the couple returned Hilary had confessed that she couldn't face giving the puppy up because she had become so attached to the little animal.

Billie currently worked several hours a day in Alexei's company and occasionally accompanied him abroad. These days he travelled less because he was keen to take an active role in his children's daily life. Billie had found her husband wonderfully supportive during her pregnancy and it had wiped out all the memories of her lonely sense of isolation while she'd carried Nicky. She had enjoyed her second pregnancy and had also been blessed with a straightforward delivery. It would be a long time before she forgot Alexei's eyes shining with tears of pride and fascination when he saw his daughter for the first time.

As Nicky pelted out of the nursery and greeted his father at the top of his voice Billie turned to greet Alexei.

'Your mother's flirting like mad with your father. He's mesmerised,' Alexei revealed with a wicked grin.

'Oh, dear, I do hope she doesn't hurt his feelings.' Billie sighed.

'I think Desmond is mature enough to look after himself,' Alexei told her with quiet assurance. 'How's our daughter?'

'Fast asleep. I think all the attention she got this afternoon exhausted her.'

'You got plenty of attention too,' Alexei reminded her, scanning her slim shapely figure in the sapphire-blue dress and jacket she wore. 'You look amazing, *agapi mou.*'

He closed his arms round Billie and eased her up against his tall, powerful body. He stared down into her shining eyes and the ready smile of welcome already tugging at her ripe mouth and murmured softly, 'Every time I see you, it's like coming home and like no other feeling I've ever had. I love you, *moraki mou.*'

Billie whispered the same sentiment back with similar intensity and gave herself up to the pleasure of his mouth on hers, happiness singing through her every skin cell…